FLIGHT
OF A
HABIT

David Barrow

TRAFFORD

• Canada • UK • Ireland • USA •

Note for Librarians: A cataloguing record for this book is available from Library
and Archives Canada at www.collectionscanada.ca/amicus/index-e.html

ISBN 1-4120-9063-6

Printed in Victoria, BC, Canada. Printed on paper with minimum 30% recycled fibre.
Trafford's print shop runs on "green energy" from solar, wind and other
environmentally-friendly power sources.

Offices in Canada, USA, Ireland and UK

Book sales for North America and international:
Trafford Publishing, 6E–2333 Government St.,
Victoria, BC V8T 4P4 CANADA
phone 250 383 6864 (toll-free 1 888 232 4444)
fax 250 383 6804; email to orders@trafford.com
Book sales in Europe:
Trafford Publishing (UK) Limited, 9 Park End Street, 2nd Floor
Oxford, UK OX1 1HH UNITED KINGDOM
phone +44 (0)1865 722 113 (local rate 0845 230 9601)
facsimile +44 (0)1865 722 868; info.uk@trafford.com
Order online at:
trafford.com/06-0819

10 9 8 7 6 5 4 3 2

Thanks and Dedication

Dedicated to
Mary, Christopher, Diana, and Jo. All have cajoeled me
into going into print!

My thanks go to Mary my wife, who apart from putting
up with me for an awful long time, has spent many hours
correcting my appalling grammar and spelling, and has
done the initial edit, with difficulty as I don't like changing
anything once I have written it!

Alan MacDougal for producing the cover from my
photographic disasters and suggestions.

Jennifer Thomas who proof read the final draft
before printing.

All at Trafford who have made it possible to publish my
'magnum opus'. We all supposedly have a book in us, this is
mine; but there seems to be another on the way!

Authors note

─────────

Cocaine is a nasty Class A drug. Those that smuggle the drug are breaking the law big time and can expect to receive the severest sentences.

Whether being used by chewing, snorting, smoking, injecting, or drinking; whatever a user may say, it is an addictive drug.

Whether it is used socially in its powder form for snorting up the nose, or the Coca leaf chewed as in South America it is still a dangerous drug, in spite of what these users may say. The other three ways are even more dangerous, with the added risks of medical problems such as lung and heart disease, or problems contracted from dirty needles.

What is cocaine? It comes from the leaves of the Coca plant - a large family, which grows well in warm wet climates such as are found in the foothills of the Andes, through Colombia, Bolivia, Brazil, and Peru. The concentration of the drug in the leaf is greater when grown at an altitude of 1000 to 5000 feet. Some varieties of the plant have a higher concentration of the drug in the leaves than others, so generally speaking, the drug is only extracted from four of the varieties. Other than the use by chewing, cocaine has to be extracted by chemical 'manufacturing'.

It was probably originally used by the local natives for

medicinal purposes many centuries ago, before these uses were discovered by the developed world late in the nineteenth century, though there is evidence that the Conquistadors traded profitably in it. It is only in the last half century that it has become an increasing problem, with fortunes being made in smuggling it to the more affluent parts of the world and governments spending millions on counter measures. The drug Cartels that have developed from the trade have escalated into all sorts of business, with money laundering, murder and every other form of crime imaginable. Drugs, or drug money, have played big parts in civil war in Central America and have affected all classes, from Presidents to the humblest farmer.

This fictional story takes a light-hearted approach to smuggling cocaine, but is in no way implying or condoning the practice of either smuggling or using the drug.

Recently in this country, since this story was written, a gang have been convicted of smuggling a large quantity of cocaine hidden inside a shipment of coconuts, and have received long sentences. Customs and Excise are ever vigilant!

It is a nasty habit and a dangerous one to have. Don't try it!

Many of the place names and locations may seem familiar, or appear on your atlas or map, but they have been used solely as a reference point and may easily not be described as you may know them, if they are sites you have visited.

All the characters in this tale are from my imagination and in no way represent any persons, living or deceased.

Chapter 1

No 9 Meadowsweet Road, as I had expected, was a semi-detached small house set in a cul-de-sac and part of an enormous new development on the northern side of Bristol. I had found it easy to find by using the A-Z, but might have had difficulty if I had had to rely on the directions given.

I pulled the MG sports up in front and rang the bell.

The house had a small front garden, neatly mown lawn with flower beds each side of the path leading up from the gate. The window to the left of the door had net curtains drawn tightly across. It all gave an impression of tidy privacy.

The door opened almost immediately as if I had been inspected as I arrived, and certainly expected.

It was some time since I had been in a similar situation. I had earlier phoned several numbers from the local newspaper; before picking this one which sounded as if it was a private house, rather than a "parlour", which would give me a more intimate and private meeting. The voice on the phone had also sounded friendly, but other than the few questions I had asked I had no idea what would be on the other side of the door.

"Hi, are you Sarah?" I asked somewhat nervously.

The girl in front of me was probably 5 foot six, brown

shoulder-length hair; at a guess late twenties, slim waist with neat firm-looking breasts, deep brown eyes, as far as I could see in the gloom of the hallway. All this was dressed in knee-length black shiny boots, black stockings, the shortest (no imagination needed) red mini skirt, a transparent mauve sleeveless top with a black bra underneath. Quite a dish, and just the distraction I had hoped for, but would suit me very well; certainly not quite what I had been expecting. I had expected someone older and not so good-looking, probably a bit worn round the edges!

I had looked in the local paper and had picked her out at random, not really believing the advert's description.

"Yes, I'm Sarah, and you must be Chris. Do you like the look of what you can see?" She asked confidently.

She spoke with a soft well-spoken voice with a distinctive accent which I immediately recognised as Irish. I should know, as I had done a tour in Northern Ireland while in the army.

"Sorry, I didn't mean to stare, but I was just eyeing up the goods before I bought them! And I think I like what I can see."

"OK thank you, the 'goods' will cost you £75 if you want the all-inclusive. That's for an hour; if you want longer we will have to negotiate. Would you like a drink before we go up? I find it helps to relax guys and we can have a chat."

She did not appear to be put out by my rather direct approach, but was probably used to all sorts of 'compliments'.

"That would be nice, tea if that's easy."

She led me to the left into the living room and I sat down on the sofa, while she went on into the open kitchen to boil a kettle. My impression of neatness of the outside of the house was carried to the inside. This room was tastefully furnished, tidy, and spotlessly clean.

While the kettle boiled she came back in and perched on an armchair. If I had been pleased with what I had seen as I

2

arrived, I was doubly so now as she exposed a large amount of thigh.

"What do you do, Chris? That's a nice car you have, so I expect you have some high-flying job."

With difficulty I dragged my eyes up to her face. I could feel my face flushing as I realised she must be aware of my excitement, but then her job was to give pleasure to her customers. .

"Well actually at the moment I don't do anything. I was in the army for 15 years but we got tired of each other and I left. The story of my life really, as I have just got my divorce through; she couldn't wait while I was away somewhere."

I wasn't going to tell her that I had recently come out of a military prison after 18 months......

This seems like a good time to tell you who I am, and about my chequered life up to this point.

My early life was quite unremarkable. Born in Essex, an only child of well-off parents (my father worked in the city); they had married rather late in life and probably found me a handful but I was refused nothing, so probably thoroughly spoilt. Aged 12 I went to Eton College where I lived for the sport and could not be bothered academically, so achieved only four 'O' levels. I never had the chance to get much further as I was caught smoking hash with my naked housemaster's daughter one afternoon when I should have been in the chemistry lab; the sort of chemistry I was indulging in was much more to my taste! So Eton and I parted company rather abruptly.

My parents promptly shipped me off to Australia to live with a distant cousin who owned a large chunk of the Northern Territories. The theory being that there would be few temptations in the Outback, and out of sight was out of mind as far as they were concerned. After a year of hard, but enjoyable, work I had saved enough money to buy a ticket back to UK, unbeknown to my parents, and joined the army aged 18.

I was 6 foot and more than capable of looking after myself, having been schooled in the Oz outback, and quickly got a reputation as someone not to be messed with by my contemporaries. After initial training I was posted to the RASC as a driver, and shortly afterwards over to Northern Ireland. Promotion came quite quickly, and after other various postings I was appointed to Catterick as a sergeant. Always short of cash, I found a ready market for army stores I sold through a local publican; eventually the word got out and my next posting was the stockade and inevitably the loss of my stripes.

Eight years before, I thought I had fallen madly in love with a girl in Aldershot, but this was quite short-lived. After we were married and during a spell in Germany she wandered and left me, much to my relief, and my enforced confinement was the final straw.

My parents had both been killed in a car accident on the M25 soon after I entered the stockade and I had inherited a large amount of money; hence the car and lifestyle. So it suited everybody that I should retire from Her Majesty's Service.

Enough of my life story. I was keen to find out more about Sarah.

We went upstairs to a small room mostly taken up with a double bed.

"Get your kit off and I will give you a massage."

As she spoke she pulled her top over her head and dropped her mini skirt to reveal a lacy bra and suspender belt holding up the black stockings, and the briefest of thongs. She leant forward to unzip the boots down the side giving me an exciting new view, followed by standing on one leg to remove her stockings. This was all that I had been looking forward to, and was more than ready to sample.

"On your front. I will start with your back."

She had exquisitely soft hands which kneaded the sweet smelling oil into my skin with a slow rhythmic circular

4

motion; if I had not been feeling so excited the firm pressure could easily have lulled me to sleep.

I turned over and she found all the special places. I reached up behind her to release her bra to unshackle her small firm perfect breasts and she slipped off the thong to give me what I had come for.

Later we lay talking.

"You have got a lovely suntan, do you use a sun bed to keep it going?"

She was a lovely even very pale golden brown all over.

"No," she laughed "I was born this colour. My father is Colombian. He came over 30 years ago, met my mother in Belfast, and I was the first of six children. I am half-Colombian and half-Irish; went to school initially in Belfast before the family moved to Preston."

"Why do you do this, don't you find it demeaning? Constantly being used by men. Surely you can't get any satisfaction from it."

"The reason I do it is for the money, I can earn more in a week doing this than I used to earn in three months as a shop assistant, and no tax to pay. I've been on the game for about two years now, and if I wish I can retire in a couple of years and get myself a nice place and settle down.

It's not demeaning, after all it is the oldest profession in the world! You are buying an hour of my time and my body. I am providing a service like many other jobs except that I am using my body as a tool, just like a baker uses his hands to make bread! Most of my clients are very pleasant so I meet a lot of different people. I won't do the more erotic things that some men enjoy so am perhaps not like the street girls or massage parlours. Some men do have a need for some relaxation and visiting me provides them with that, I aim to give a really quality service. I do not feel ashamed at what I do but society does frown on it and so I do not admit to friends or family that this is how I earn a living.

5

I don't have a boyfriend at present so it sometimes gives me satisfaction sexually as well."

"Do you do drugs? Is that why you need a lot of money? Though you certainly don't look as if you do."

"No. Certainly not. I have never done drugs and think it a waste of money and I should hate to become dependent on them. I can understand those that have got to that state, though, and must have them. Of course a lot of girls in this line of business do work to feed their habit."

"Do you rent this house, and what does your landlord think about it?"

"You ask a lot of questions. Are you a policeman really, or a journalist?"

She said this as if she was becoming slightly worried and annoyed at my questioning.

"No, just interested to know what makes you girls tick. It's not the job that many girls would want to do. As a matter of interest do the police give you any hassle?"

"OK, I will continue to answer your questions. I suppose they are quite harmless! Actually, I have a couple of policemen who are my clients. The police are not worried about small places like this, as they cause no trouble and are very discreet. What they do dislike are the girls on the street; the pimps that inevitably go with them and the crime etc. that follows.

I am my own landlady. The house belongs to me and the building society. I rented this house to start with for the first year. My then landlady knew what I did; she has another house where she works in the same way. You see there is a good living to be made!

Now you must go, as I have another gentleman coming in half an hour. If you want to ask me more questions you will have to come again. I have enjoyed meeting you and our chat. I hope you now understand what makes me tick!"

I left feeling really good and was sure I would be back

again. A chap has to have some pleasures in life! It had been money well spent.

I felt there was a lot more to Sarah than was first evident; I sensed she was an intelligent girl who had thought out how she could best advance herself in life with the assets she had, and she certainly had some very good assets from where I had been lying!

Chapter 2

Over the next few weeks I paid regular visits to Meadowsweet Road and, apart from the obvious delights, I began to really look forward to seeing Sarah for what she was as a person. Our relationship became no longer "business" but one of a growing friendship. I was no longer just another punter and Sarah admitted that she looked forward to and enjoyed my company in the same way.

We started going out to the pub for a drink in the evening, and then it was 'takeaways' back to No.9. followed by spending weekends together usually at my house, with long country walks, cosy evenings round the fire, or both busy in my garden. We got to know each other much better and were no longer reticent about ourselves and families; we discovered that we had many interest in common, particularly of wide open spaces and getting away from the clutter of crowds.

The only fly in the ointment was Sarah's profession: I was beginning to wish, as I got to know her better, that she earned her living in some more conventional way. I suppose I was vaguely jealous of the other men in her life, who wouldn't be? Although I realised that they were of no importance to her and once out of her front door were forgotten. However, this was one topic we did not discuss.

I discovered in the course of our growing friendship and conversations that Colleen—Sarah was her working name—was born in Belfast of a Colombian father, Juan Gonzales, who had come to the UK early in the '70s and got work as a labourer in the Belfast shipyard; her mother was born, bred and brought up as a staunch Catholic in Belfast. The family, while IRA sympathisers, were not active in the movement.

Juan had had a stormy "courtship" with the Irish family, who were not so keen on their daughter falling in love with a Colombian, which was not considered right for a good Irish girl, in spite of the fact he was improving himself by attending night school regularly. The fact that he was a Catholic, though slightly slipped, was one point in his favour. Love prevailed and Colleen's parents married, and she was the first born within a year. It sounded as if Colleen was always given all the encouragement she needed to improve her educational standard, both at school in Belfast and when the family moved to Preston in Lancashire, when her father got a manager's job in a small factory. She left school with three 'A' levels in French, Spanish, and Italian. A bright girl, as I had thought from the beginning, and quite different from my lack of academic achievement.

Finding work to make use of her language talents seemed impossible, and she eventually got fed up with a succession of low-paid shop assistant jobs that were going to get her nowhere. She was a girl of great determination who could not wait to achieve in life, and realised that money was the way to do it. I could sense sometimes her frustration at my idle laid back approach to everything.

A friend, one evening, jokingly suggested that the only way to make money was to become a "working girl" and go on the game. Colleen, on reflection, decided "why not?" she was not exactly a complete novice, having had several relationships since leaving school, and she was not a practising Catholic so there never had been a problem at confession! She did want to get on in life and money was the

9

fuel to enable her to do this. On more reflection she decided that she needed to be working at the top end of the market rather than walking the streets, offering a discreet private service and at a higher price. Quality was the name of the game; her looks and outgoing personality meant that this was easily achieved, as I had discovered the first time we had met.

Obviously she needed to get away from the Preston area, as it would not do to have acquaintances arriving on her doorstep as punters! So the move was made to Bristol into a rented house, on the pretext to her family that she had secured a good job. I came on the scene two years later, by which time she had been able to put down the deposit and secure the mortgage on No 9 Meadowsweet Road.

Our relationship continued to develop to the extent that I was never a paying customer. She continued her business during the day, and we would meet up in the evenings as a normal couple. I had secured myself a job as a lorry driver (to keep myself out of mischief, but really egged on by Colleen to do something useful.) and was often away for several days at a time. My time in the army with the RASC as a driver made it easy to find a good but not highly paid job, but money was not of great importance to me, thanks to my inheritance.

I had a licence that allowed me to drive the biggest of articulated lorries and was good at the job. I enjoyed driving, but the monotony of trundling along at 58 mph often covering the same route several times a week, the increasing traffic congestion and the appalling standard of driving by some of the public began to get to me, and I realised that this was not what I wanted from life. I was becoming increasingly bored with the job and, looking for rather more adventure in my life.

My thoughts turned to seeing more of the world by taking time out to travel. Thanks to my inheritance from my parents money was no problem, but I did not feel that I could go through life with no goal ahead of me. A year out travelling might lead to some opportunity or, at the least, ideas.

Did I want to travel on my own? There were advantages such as being a totally free agent, and one would meet people along the way. On the other hand what about my relationship with Colleen? If I went alone then the chances were that I would have lost her, and this was something that I was reluctant to have happen. One or other of us would be bound to meet someone else. The next logical thought was to see if she would travel with me. She was very keen on making money from her business and might think time out was not achieving this goal. I continued to ponder on the subject for several days while I spent endless hours on the motorways—often stationary! At last I decided the only sensible way was to broach the subject with Colleen and find out whether she would come with me, but whatever the reply, I would go.

The next evening, being a weekend, when I returned home and we were enjoying a ham salad and baked potatoes washed down with a very nice Chilean Chardonnay, I brought the subject up.

"I am pretty fed up with this driving; it's so boring. I don't feel I am getting anywhere with my life. I have been thinking about it quite a lot over the last few weeks and have decided to go abroad for a while."

This was fairly blunt, and obviously came very much out of the blue for Colleen.

"Oh, I see. What will you do and where do you plan on going?"

I got the feeling that she was vaguely disappointed, but perhaps that was my imagination or wishful thinking.

"I haven't thought that bit out yet, except I would like to travel. I think probably I would go to the States or Canada, or perhaps up into Alaska initially. Move around a bit but also possibly work somewhere if the opportunity arose and I liked the place. Would you like to come with me?"

11

Now I had said it. I subconsciously held my breath waiting to see her reaction. This was the moment of truth. If she said no, would I really go; or would I make some excuse to myself to stay; or would I be strong-minded, as I intended and sever our relationship. The other faint possibility was that I went and was then able to persuade her to join me later, but that depended entirely on her feelings about me.

"That's quite a decision for a girl to make in a hurry! But yes please! Where should we go and when?"

Her eyes had lit up and, if it had not been for the ham salad on our knees, I would have given her a big hug. She had had no hesitation in her answer, which was a good boost for my confidence and I can't tell you how relieved I was.

"That's really good. We will have such fun. The world is our oyster, we can be as free as the wind, go when and where we want. Have you thought with your impetuosity, at all about your business and wish to make quick money?"

"Oh that can wait. I can come back to it if I want or start up in another country." She said with a twinkle in her eye.

"Let's sleep on it and we may come up with some bright ideas of where we want to go. I still quite like the sound of Alaska but am open to any suggestion. I really don't mind. I am really just so glad you said yes."

Early the next morning, a Sunday, so I was enjoying the feeling of no rush to get on the road and able to enjoy a lie in, I was awakened by a good shaking.

"I've got it sorted." Colleen said, sitting on the edge of the bed beside me.

"For heaven's sake what are you on about at this hour?" I replied grumpily.

"Our travels: I know where we should go first."

"OK, let's have it and then I can get back to sleep."

"Colombia. We can go and visit my mystery uncle who I have never met."

This brought me fully awake and we started to make plans: The first thing was to get in touch with the Gonzales tribe, which Colleen had never really mentioned, other than that she had an uncle and cousins in Colombia. In a long phone call later to her parents, she was able to drag out of her father an address and phone number for the family in Bogota. Later that morning, with this information she phoned her uncle. Yes, they would be delighted to have us to stay in Bogota for as long as we wished. Colleen had no idea whether they lived in a mansion or a slum, as the brothers Juan and Fredericko had fallen out when Juan left, 30 odd years before, and had not spoken since. Juan's early life had always been a taboo subject in Colleen's upbringing and she had very little idea about her Colombian roots other than that they existed.

I gave in my notice to the haulage firm; Colleen stopped taking bookings and cancelled her regular customers (all much to my satisfaction); plane tickets were booked, and six weeks later found us at Heathrow having let Colleen's house in Bristol through a letting agent for a year, and my house in the Cotswolds I had shut up, and arranged for a good neighbour to look in periodically to keep an eye on it. We were free to travel the world as we wished with no ties to anybody or anything.

As usual with flying the journey was tedious, but it was the only way to get from A to B with as little hassle as possible. As we went through the formalities of customs and immigration at Bogota, Colleen became more and more nervous about meeting her new relations. I could understand that it was a big step to be taking, and for the whole flight had been trying to boost her morale. The nearer we got to the exit the more delays she found to put off the moment. This was not the self-confident girl I had first met!

She need not have worried. As we emerged from the bowels of the arrivals, we could not miss the enormous banner being held up by two young men in their mid twenties: "Welcome to our cousin Colleen". This looked like a good start, anyway. The smile came back on Colleen's face as she saw it.

The relief to me was that they both spoke some English and introduced themselves as Pedro and Rogero, the sons of Fredericko who was devastated that he had been unable to come to greet his niece in person, but his business required him.

We were ushered out to a large black Buick car; our rucksacks put in the boot by the porter who seemed to appear at the click of Rogero's fingers. Colleen, as you can imagine, never a shy girl, was a different person from a few minutes before. Getting going pretty well with her schoolgirl Spanish, I could see she was loving every minute of the attention being given her. Pedro got in the driving seat, and we were off on what became a wild drive through heavy traffic towards the centre of the city. Half an hour later we pulled up in front of the main door of a large imposing mini skyscraper office block in downtown Bogota.

"Here we will meet with my father, before we take you home." explained Rogero.

I had not yet sorted out which of the boys was the eldest; Rogero seemed to be the more dominant of the two, but Pedro seemed to have taken an immediate shine to his beautiful cousin. Colleen was certainly looking radiant and I mentally thanked my luck at having arrived on her doorstep those weeks ago.

"What is your father's business?" I asked tentatively of Pedro as we were led into the lift and whisked upwards.

"He has an import and export business. Rogero and I are also in the business."

"Will our bags be OK left in the car. I did not see it locked and I hear there is quite a lot of crime in Colombia", I asked rather belatedly, hoping that I was not sounding like a British fusspot.

"Don't worry about that. They are quite safe in our car. The security at the door will look after it."

I had not taken a lot of notice in the lift as to which floor we were headed, but it seemed a long way up. I decided we must be at the top floor, as the lift doors opened to reveal a large sumptuous reception area with soft pastel-painted walls hung with colourful oil paintings discreetly lit by overhead spot lights. On the right was a large, completely clear desk, except for a newspaper, with a tough heavily built looking man behind it who was on his feet and came round the desk as the lift doors opened. Straight in front of the lift doors, across the deep piled carpet, stood another desk with a most attractive dark-haired well-dressed girl behind it. This desk was in complete contrast to the other, with a bank of telephones and a computer screen and the usual clutter of papers, except it was a very tidy clutter, if there can be such a thing.

"Hey, Francesca, Mick, this is our cousin from England," shouted Pedro, as we walked across towards a solid-looking door to the left of the secretary's desk. Before we could reach it, the door swung open.

"What is all this noise and shouting going on in here?"

A broad-shouldered medium height man of about 55, with greying swept-back oiled hair and wearing an expensive silk suit with a red carnation in the buttonhole, appeared through the door.

As Colleen stepped out from behind Pedro, the suited man threw wide his arms and embraced Colleen in a bear hug. At last holding her at arms length,

"My little niece, my Colleen."

"Uncle Fredericko?" Colleen was just able to get out rather breathlessly after the enormous bear hug.

"Why have you never been to see us before, my little bebe?"

Without waiting for a reply he turned towards me, still with his arm round Colleen's shoulders, and stuck out his hand, much to my relief as I thought I might also be the recipient of a hug.

"And you must be Christoph." His handshake felt it was enough to break the bones, but I gave nearly as good as he. The shake was held for a moment, as we looked each other straight in the eye, both appraising each other. This was a man one would either like a lot and respect, or could easily be cowed by. At this moment I was not sure which direction my thoughts would go, but I tightened my grasp and was not going to be awed by this first meeting. What was quite plain was that he was a very strong character and very definitely head of the family, as the two boys had become quiet in his presence.

Turning away from me he again held Colleen at arm's length with both hands on her shoulders.

"How could that brother of mine have possibly produced such a lovely flower! It must have come from the Irish side of your family."

Colleen definitely had scored plenty of points with the first meeting! I could see she was rather overawed by his greeting but at the same time obviously enjoying every minute of it.

"Enough. You must be tired after your journey. Rogero, take them home and introduce them to Mama and then come back here. Pedro, you stay, we have some business to discuss. I will see you later when you have rested."

I wondered what Colleen was really thinking about all this effusive greeting. It was all quite a lot to take in a short time.

Chapter 3

We were driven by Rogero back out into the suburbs. I had totally lost my sense of direction, so was unsure where we were other than arriving at some very impressive high metal gates set in a long wall, topped with blue glazed tiles, stretching away to each side. The gates were attended by two suited young men who looked very like guards of some sort to me. My information that Bogota was a dangerous place was I felt born out, but then Colombia was renowned for its drug cartels and crime of all descriptions.

The gates swung open as Rogero leaned out of the window and greeted the guards, obviously explaining who we were at the same time. It seemed that everybody had to be checked in.

In front of the car stretched a long tree-lined shady drive, with well kept lawns and beds of colourful shrubs and flowers leading up in a great swathe to a big white colonial style house with balconies running round both the ground and first floors; the sort of design that one had seen in films centred on the deep south of the US. It looked expensive, and the kind of house I would have expected Uncle Fredericko to have, having just met him. Though certainly not what I had been imagining.

"Come on in and meet Mama. Don't worry about your

17

bags. They will be taken up to your rooms," shouted Pedro as he leapt out of the car. He seemed to be full of boundless energy except when in the presence of his father. Personally, just at the moment I was feeling somewhat jaded after a long overnight flight.

As we got out of the car a woman of probably nearly six foot came out of the front door on to the stoop.

She was, I should think about fifty, but it was difficult to tell as she was extremely elegant and as a younger woman must have been a real beauty. She was simply dressed in a pale green dress which complimented her auburn hair to perfection.

"Mama, this is Colleen our cousin, and Christoph her friend."

Mama came down the steps to greet us. Colleen, not with a Fredericko hug, but with a gentle embrace and kiss on each cheek. I just got a friendly handshake, more's the pity!

"Welcome, my dears, to our home. It is lovely to meet you at long last. We have so much to talk about and find out about our families. But first you must have a little siesta and freshen up, you must be tired after your journey. I always find flying so tedious. Would you like a juice or something first?"

She had a most attractive, I think French, accent with all the poise of a well-schooled upbringing.

Colleen and I had had great discussions prior to leaving the UK, and on the plane, about the Colombian family. It seemed that Colleen's father and Fredericko had fallen out in a big way which was why Juan had come to England years ago. As a child growing up in Belfast, and later Preston, the Colombian connection had been a taboo subject and was never mentioned. All she knew was that her father had come from a poor family with minimal education and means.

This was no poor family, Fredericko had obviously prospered in the intervening years, but we would no doubt discover more during our stay.

We were shown to two adjoining rooms at the back of the

house, looking out over more shady, beautifully manicured gardens with oranges and other fruit trees at the far end a hundred yards away.

Set amongst them were three or four cottages and what I took to be garages and other outbuildings.

On the left of the house as I looked out was a patio area and swimming pool surrounded with comfortable looking loungers and umbrellas. The whole garden looked as if it was enclosed by the wall we had seen by the front gates.

My room was lavishly furnished with a deep carpet and rather heavy furniture, a king-size double bed with what I took to be a mosquito net ready to be pulled round it. The whole room was decorated in subtle shades of pale blue. I'm not much of an expert on interior design but to my eye this looked pretty good. The bathroom led straight off it, and had a large ornate bath and shower etc. The whole suite was all very comfortable. My rucksack was already in my room, and had even been unpacked, I was not sure that my rather tatty and creased clothes were up to standard. So the service was good as well!

I knocked on Colleen's door and was let in immediately. Colleen's room was similar to mine but in a more feminine way and decorated in pinks.

"Cor, it's all a bit grand, isn't it! You should have contacted your relations years ago. Should I have brought my dinner jacket for the evening do you think!? I liked Mama, she was really welcoming."

"Yes she seems really nice. But don't be so silly. We could only have brought our travelling clothes and hadn't expected such luxury. So it's too bad. I am going to have a shower and sleep, as Mama suggested, and see if I can borrow an iron to make my only dress less creased."

I enjoyed soaking in a deep refreshing bath, but found I was tired but not sleepy and settled for looking through the pile of magazines on the bedside table, though they were all written in Spanish, of course, which was not a lot of use to me.

I suppose I must have dropped off, as three hours later Colleen appeared at my window having walked along the balcony. Apparently on asking about an iron, a maid had appeared and taken the dress away to return shortly with it perfectly pressed. We should make the most of this five star treatment while we were here as I was certain we would not encounter it again during our travels.

"I think we should dress as best we can for supper and go down to face the family, as it's getting late and they probably didn't like to wake us." I decided she was finding it rather daunting being plunged in at the deep end with so many of her new family.

Twenty minutes later we made our entrance. We need not have worried about dress as the men were all in casual slacks and shirts, while Mama had changed into another simple but stunning dress that I am sure was the height of Paris fashion. The men had apparently returned from the office an hour ago; we were immediately made most welcome with long cool drinks, and I could see Colleen relaxing by the minute.

Fredericko did tend to have a rather overbearing personality but I could see that Mama, I never did discover her name, was a very good catalyst to him and seemed in the house definitely to be the dominant one.

Over the delicious three-course supper, waited on by a maid and manservant, I sat next to Mama and learned that she came from an old French family; I had been correct in my first assumption about her accent. She had been brought up in what is now called Guyana, but had up to 1966 been French Guiana, more recently well known for the penal colony, and the book Papillon, on the north east corner of the continent bordering Brazil. She was able to trace her family right back to the first disastrous settlement in 1763. Her family business was still in sugar and Cayenne pepper.

After dinner I found it much more difficult to learn Fredericko's family past. I am a great one for asking questions as Colleen had pointed out when I had first met her. Fredericko was slightly more forthcoming about his business and I soon discovered that he was involved in buying and selling coffee and rubber, but dabbled in local handicrafts, all of which were exported to the USA and Europe principally.

"And what do you do, Christoph, when not travelling the world?"

I explained that I had been in the army with whom I had had a disagreement, and spent some time in a military prison, which seemed to amuse him (I can't think why I should have admitted this to him), before inheriting some money and just doing a lorry driver's job for some time. I was quite surprised at myself opening up to this man who was really a stranger to me and whom as yet I hadn't felt quite comfortable with.

We seemed to get on quite well and, in spite of my reservations on first meeting him, I felt that provided I stood up to him we could have a reasonable relationship, though his next question came as a bit of a surprise out of the blue.

"What are your intentions towards my niece?" This asked with a twinkle in his eye and a glance towards Colleen to make sure she was not within earshot.

This was not the sort of question that I would have expected from an uncle at the first time of meeting. I hesitated only a moment, but had time to begin to feel slight anger that he should be prying into our relationship after such a short acquaintance.

"We are just good friends who have decided to see the world together. In England we have become much more relaxed about this sort of thing. I don't see that it is something I have to explain to her uncle though. She is a big girl now and I can assure you more than capable of looking after herself."

I said this in as polite a way as possible with a wide smile, but thought for a moment he was going to explode. He was obviously not used to being answered back. However, his frown changed in a moment to a bellow of laughter. This did make me warm to him somewhat. I felt that it had been the right answer to give him and had probably scored me quite a lot of points in his estimation.

"I like that, Christoph, I like that."

The others, who had been all talking together, looked over to us and their conversation stopped at the outburst, and we all joined up together.

"I hope you have not been grilling Cris?" asked Mama.

"Would I do such a thing!" replied Fredericko with a large smile. Mama's look said it all, she knew him too well.

"What have you been telling Uncle Fredericko about me, Cris? I am sure he was trying to find out the story of my life!"

"Only telling him of all your bad habits." I said, with a smile and a large wink.

"I am sure she has none." This from Pedro who was obviously rather smitten with his attractive new cousin.

Little did he know what a bad girl she was! I must at the first chance find out what story she was telling everybody. This was something we had not thought of discussing before hand but we had not known what the family were going to be like. It could lead to a lot of embarrassment if we had conflicting stories.

The evening drew to a close on a convivial note, and I certainly was now ready to crash out like a light.

Chapter 4

Over breakfast the next morning the discussion turned to the plans for our stay in Colombia.

Colleen and I had only thought about it very generally as we'd had no idea what reception we would get from the family. Our further plans were equally vague, other than we had thought of travelling down through South America as circumstances took us, so we had no timetable to keep to, and had imagined that we would just stop wherever we took a liking to. We had never envisaged staying more than a few days with the Gonzales, but that was not to be.

Fredericko took charge, as one might have expected.

"We will make all arrangements for you while you are in Colombia and you will treat our home as yours. One of the boys will travel with you at all times and you only have to tell him what you wish to do. I suggest you put your heads together and sort it all out. Rogero, you are not busy for the next few days so you look after them."

Pedro looked slightly disappointed at this order. It was a definite order too, no doubt about that!

The three of us got together in the living room while Pedro drove his father to the office.

"OK, what's it to be then?"

"Have you any suggestions of where we should go, and what to see?" Colleen asked.

Eventually we came up with an itinerary of a sort. We would have two days in Bogota to see the sights and learn about the history of Colombia, before making a trip out to the Pacific coast, and then inland to the Rain Forest.

The city was not as interesting as we had hoped, but then that sort of thing was not quite our scene. Dominated by two fine churches and having some attractive Plazas, with crusty old men; shoulders and heads covered in pigeon poo, standing on plinths; statues, of course, of the famous of yesteryear.

As with most large cities there was great variation between the business area and the inevitable poor slum parts, though I am sure Rogero did not take us to the really deprived areas.

The whole city lying on the gently sloping foothills of the Eastern Cordillera which are the northern end of the great Andes chain. We were at over 8000 feet in a very pleasant temperate climate. All in all a very nice place to live, although for the first couple of days we did feel rather lethargic from the effects of the altitude. Neither Colleen nor I are great city lovers and after a leisurely day and a half we had had enough. Rogero suggested that we pay a visit to the family warehouse out on an industrial site. A large concrete building that looked impregnable and proved to be just so, until the guard checked us out on a hidden CCTV before releasing the wicket gate.

"Is this level of security really necessary?" I asked Rogero with some surprise.

"Yes, we have some valuable merchandise stored here which many people would like to take for their own if we don't protect it, so we have to have the best surveillance that we can buy and guards here all the time."

On entering into the main storage area we were assailed by the wonderful smell of coffee beans and faced with

24

mountains of high stacked sacks. Further on were piles of rubber made into blocks.

"This all gets shipped down to the port at Barranquilla by lorry or train before being exported mainly to the States and some to Europe," explained Rogero.

"Who are you buying your stocks from? I assume you are acting as agents."

"Yes, we buy direct from the farmers or their cooperative groups. We have agents working for us who travel round the country. Sometimes we are buying just a few kilos, and others many tonnes."

I still felt rather surprised that such bulky commodities as coffee and rubber warranted such a high security level, but decided it would be tactless to enquire any further. Perhaps the handicrafts that Fredericko had mentioned were stored here as well and were more valuable, but there was no mention of these and no evidence of them in the warehouse.

Later, when Colleen and I were having a pre supper chat in my room, I brought the subject up again with her.

"Do you get the feeling that there is something about the family business which we have not been told? And the guards on the warehouse and the gates here. The family seems to be very respected and feared. Colombia does have a reputation for exporting other things as well that are not quite so well received abroad, you know."

I was really just speaking my musings out loud, probably rather stupidly.

"Don't be ridiculous, Cris. What are you suggesting? How can you be so ungrateful when they have been so kind to us. They are my family." And with a jibe below the belt; "Just because of your criminal past you think you can see something suspicious."

I could see that I had really said the wrong thing as Colleen was about to let fly at me. I had only once been the recipient of a tongue lashing from her which had become quite violent for a while, so was not keen to goad her any further now.

"OK, I am sorry. I am very appreciative of their kindness. As you know I have an inquisitive mind and have in the past been into slightly dodgy enterprises! I should just like to know more if there is more to know."

This seemed to cool her down somewhat, but I wondered to myself if she had been having similar thoughts, but I wouldn't dare ask, not yet, anyhow!

Chapter 5

We were to be joined for the trip down to the Pacific by Rogero's girl friend, Juanita. She was a tall classically beautiful black-haired, slim Spanish-featured girl of 22. Her English was excellent as she was educated in the States, but still spoke with a marked accent and a sexy husky voice. She was easy to get on with and immediately struck up a friendship with Colleen.

The four of us set off the next morning in the Buick, heading down towards the coast near Buenaventura, with the plan to drive on south down the coast in no hurry and to stop wherever the attractions took us. The trouble with this was that Colleen and I were very definitely country people whereas Rogero and Juanita felt deprived if they did not have access to bars, night-clubs, and city life in general. They needed people round them all the time. I could see that after a few days one or other of the couples was going to feel bored.

The drive down to the coast was magnificent, following the excellent main road with the towering snowcapped mountains looking like jagged iced cakes on each side, while the road clung to the mountainside with precipitous drops below; steep twisting turns and wonderful views of remote valleys, which the road curled down into amongst the fertile fields before climbing up again to the next ridge of mountains. The valleys were scattered with small groups of buildings some of them clinging to the precipitous sides of the mountains or the banks of the rushing torrents streaming off the slopes. The fields were small, stone walled, and obviously hand cultivated with what looked like potatoes or other vegetables; occasionally there was a llama tethered on an unenclosed bit of land.

Rogero and Juanita were not keen to stop and explore with the excuse that we had a long drive and needed to get to the coast. Colleen and I would have been very happy to have had a wander amongst the fields.

We soon found a suitable hotel twenty miles south of Buenaventura which appeared to have the 'townies' necessities, anyway to keep them happy for a few days, and we felt we could survive by walking along the spectacular coastline. During the day we went our separate ways but met up in the evening for dinner and entertainment. Colleen and I did find some lovely places by taking a local bus and then just exploring, usually with a midday snack at some little bar, chatting to the natives.

It was on the second evening sitting in a restaurant on the waterfront that Rogero met a business acquaintance and went over to join him at his table for a while.

"Here, try some of this." He said on his return, passing across a small paper wrapped package.

"What is it?" I asked rather innocently, but having suspicions as I had seen similar in London clubs.

"Coke. We use it quite regularly when we are out in the evening. It gives us a real buzz to enjoy the dancing and the lovemaking later," he said with a smile. "Have you not tried it in England? It really adds another dimension to making love. Doesn't it darling?" He turned and took Juanita's hand in his on her thigh, which was well exposed as she was wearing a mini skirt and off the shoulder top and looking ravishing.

"No, we personally don't use it and we are just good

friends travelling together, and not lovers." I added just to get the record straight. I did not elaborate any further as to the relationship between Colleen and myself! Which was a strange one anyway, as I was no longer a punter but we did have sex when the need was there for us (which we both enjoyed), but without the encumbrance of love. I did not think for a moment that they believed what I was saying but that really didn't matter to me.

"Not for me, thank you. Do you want to try it Colleen?"

"I never have and I don't think I want to start now, thanks," I was rather relieved to hear her reply which was what I had expected her to say, "but you two go ahead if you want."

Rogero undid the twist of paper to reveal the white powder lying in a small heap. He shook out a small line of the powder on to his serviette and passed it to Juanita who, raising it to her nose, inhaled it up each nostril with a delicate sniff or snort. Rogero laid out another line and did the same. This they did quite openly. Apparently there was no control on the taking of cocaine as there was at home.

While we had all been enjoying an evening of drinks and laughter and dancing before, I could soon detect in Rogero and Juanita an extra sparkle and zip. Their laughter was louder and longer, their dancing was wilder and more energetic, and they both had a slightly glazed look as if they were not quite on the planet. This seemed to last for probably 40 minutes before they came back down to earth.

"That was good, man!" Rogero said, embracing Juanita passionately. These Latins certainly had few inhibitions about behaviour and blatantly using coke so publicly. I hoped that they didn't regard us British as being very stuffy!

Rogero and I started talking when he had prised himself away from Juanita and the girls had gone off to the loo.

"You seemed to get the coke very easily from your business friend; is it widely available?"

"Oh yes, it is easy if you know the dealers, which I do.

We do quite a lot of business with them and they trust my family. They know that we have friends in the police and government."

He turned the conversation to other things and I almost had the feeling that he'd realised that perhaps he had said more than he should on the subject. My suspicious mind again, but this time I wouldn't make the mistake of airing my thoughts to Colleen.

A couple of days later Colleen and I began to get itchy to get away from this scene and into the wider world, which was after all our idea for travelling in the first place. We, with Rogero's help, found a party who were to trek into the interior to see Colombian life in the raw; visit villages off the beaten track, see ruins of ancient civilisation, not to mention the teaming wildlife of the rainforest.

This was an organised trip with a local guide and we would be away for three weeks. It sounded just the thing we would enjoy, but would be quite energetic and we would be roughing it a bit. The plan was for Rogero and Juanita to return to Bogota, and we would make our own way back on our return from the jungle.

Chapter 6

We had five days to fill in before the trip started, so we said our goodbyes to the other two and caught a bus a short way up the coast to a small village where we found ourselves lodgings in a rather seedy guest house; perfectly adequate for our purposes, and a good break in for the camping we would be doing on the trip. The village amounted to very little, just off the main road so not plagued with the heavy traffic that thundered up and down it day and night. The houses, two shops, and one bar/café mostly fronted onto the soft sandy beach with brightly coloured fishing boats pulled well up on it. This was an ideal place for us to relax and do our own thing after the luxury of the Gonzales house and the frenetic life style that Rogero and Juanita enjoyed.

At the end of this stay we caught an early bus back into town, packed with an assortment of people, from those with produce to sell in the market, to a couple of well dressed girls off to office jobs. We treated ourselves to a taxi to take us to the rendezvous for the beginning of the 'jungle exploration' on the edge of town.

This proved to be a bar in the run-down suburbs of town. We were a little bit early, but having sat over coffee for an hour we did begin to wonder if we were at the right place. Shortly after Colleen had checked with the barman, a short tanned girl wearing khaki shirt and trousers and a very big pack on her back, slouch hat pushed well back and a big smile, plonked herself down next to us with a sigh of relief.

"Gooday." The accent was pure Aussie. "You look as if you are making the trek into the jungle too?"

"Yes, we are Cris and Colleen." We both replied at the same time.

"You look as if you could do with a drink." I said as she shrugged out of her rucksack.

"Oh thanks, that would be just great. A coffee would do just fine. I'm Dom by the way."

The next couple of weeks was going to be quite different to the pampered life we had got used to since arriving in Colombia.

Twenty minutes later a battered VW minibus pulled up in the road in front of the rendezvous bar where we sat sitting over our empty coffee cups on the pavement. It disgorged five people one of whom was obviously a local. The others had packs like ours so we guessed this was the rest of our party.

The trek was organised from a small office in Buenaventura by a friend of the Gonzales family, but then everybody seemed to be a friend of the family.

The VW was piled high on its roof with what looked like tents and other basic camping needs. We already had most of the equipment that was needed, such as rucksacks, sleeping bags, walking boots, ponchos, waterproofs, insect repellent, and plenty of enthusiasm. Everything else appeared to be supplied by Carlos, who was to be the guide.

Carlos was a swarthy, muscular little man with a permanently fixed smile on his face, an unruly crop of black hair and of indeterminate age, but probably in his mid forties. I reckoned that he was probably half a native Indian of these parts and so should know his way around in the forest. The extent of his English seemed to be 'OK', but he obviously took a great liking to Colleen, and his smile broadened (if that were possible) as soon as he realised she spoke Spanish, though I gathered her 'A' level Spanish was not quite the same as his local dialect; they were able to understand each other adequately, which was some relief to me.

The four others for our fortnight's trip into the wild consisted of Peter and Marie-Louise from near Frankfurt in Germany. They were in their early twenties, newly engaged, and to be married the following year. They had both qualified recently: Peter as an industrial chemist and Marie as a pharmacist, having met at university in Bonn. They were both small and thin, but not wiry, so I hoped that they were going to be fit enough for what I suspected would be quite an arduous time in high humidity conditions. They were quiet and stuck close together as if they were rather shy and unsure of themselves.

Joanne was quite the opposite, being a big blond girl in all respects; butch, though not fat. She hailed from Kansas City in the United States of America, and we were not going to be allowed to forget it! First impressions were that she would drive us all mad within hours with her continual talking. We very quickly gathered that she was twenty and had recently finished at college, studying sociology, and was here because she was interested in local people and customs. I looked forward to seeing how her makeup would survive in the rain and heat!

Marco, from Bilbao in northern Spain, was probably about thirty, did something in finance for a living and was an avid walker and 'explorer'; I took a liking to him straight away and felt he would be a definite asset to the party. He was at least six foot, well built and extremely fit-looking.

Finally, but not least, was the Aussie girl called Dominique, "Call me Dom, please." Dom was a typical outgoing free-speaking Australian of Greek descent. I could see from the first that she would be the life and soul of the party and keep us all laughing as she poked fun at herself and us. Joanne would have to loosen up a bit if she was not to take the

33

brunt of Dom's teasing; I hoped that the two of them would not come to blows! Dom was twenty-five, a qualified nurse travelling round the world, working when she needed more funds, and out to really enjoy herself in between. A free spirit as Colleen and I planned to be.

So we were an international party who set off from Buenaventura the next morning, in the battered VW minibus driven by Carlos; having stayed the night in rooms at the rendezvous bar.

Colleen and I had already experienced the hazards of driving in Colombia on the journey down from Bogota with Rogero, when we had some pretty scary moments, and he had proved to be quite a good driver! Carlos did not fit into that category. After a short while we got off the tarmac onto dirt roads which were only wide enough for one and a half vehicles. Consequently, each time we met an oncoming car, someone had to give way and it seemed to be a matter of pride to Carlos that it would not be him. We all just prayed that the other driver would pull over before we actually made contact, the exception being lorries and buses. Carlos did recognise that these were bigger than us, and at the last moment had to give way with much shouting at the other driver and waving with both hands off the wheel.

We were quite laden down with eight of us plus rucksacks, tents, and supplies, and the VW began to show its age when we started to climb up away from the coastal plain into the foothills. Initially we were driving through mile after mile of sugar-cane fields with the height of the crop standing well above the minibus so restricting the view. As we got higher the views improved, over rolling pastureland dotted with mostly small farms with the occasional big 'estancia' stocked with masses of beef cattle. As we climbed higher it was a relief in the cramped van that the heat of the coast was left behind.

We stopped for the night in good time to pitch the tents at a small estancia that belonged to a "cousin" of Carlos.

We had discussed on the way up the division of duties, as this was very much a hands-on type of trip with everyone mucking in together for cooking etc. Peter and Marie had volunteered to get the supper this first night and made a very good job of it.

Sitting round the fire after supper, sipping the local firewater, the conversation was pretty general as we all got to know each other better. It was important being so much in one another's pockets that we got on well together. Inevitably, we started talking about the trip and our expectations of it and asking Carlos about life in Colombia.

"There is a lot of crime and murder in the country, isn't there?" asked Joanne.

"Yes I'm afraid so," replied Carlos hesitantly in his broken English, "but perhaps no more so than in your big cities in the US. This is of course where the drugs are grown and processed.

We do also have a history of violence throughout the country, particularly at times of elections due to people's different ideas of politics. In the not so distant past we have had coups and wars between the people's armies, paramilitaries and the government forces. Many, many people have been killed.

Many of us are Latin people and hot blooded, and become worked up very easily over trivial matters.

Now as well there are fights between the drug cartels and the army who are supported by your Drug Enforcement Agency."

Parts of this were spoken in Spanish and translated as best they could by Colleen and Marco.

"What about the drugs," asked Dom, "are they grown in the area we will be trekking through, and is that just cocaine?"

"We will not see coca being grown, as the fields are hidden away in the forest where the authorities cannot find them. If they do, they are destroyed by spraying with weedkillers, the bigger fields by aerial spraying which is sometimes on the wrong crop and thus bad for the farmers, who don't then have a crop to sell and so get poorer. Coca is the main drug grown, but in the past there were more of the others grown, such as marijuana and poppies for heroin and, of course, tobacco. The growing of cocaine is much more profitable than the growing of ordinary crops."

This he said as he rolled tobacco for a cigarette and lit up in a cloud of foul-smelling smoke, all with the inevitable broad smile.

"There are also the medicinal drugs such as quinine, and the many remedies for all sorts of diseases that can be extracted from the forest plants. These are the good things that we should be concentrating on."

"We read from time to time about kidnapping" I commented. "Does it happen much or is it just news when it gets in the foreign press, or when it concerns someone from one's own country?"

"I'm afraid it does happen in certain parts of the country, though down here it is not usual," Carlos added quickly, as he saw the look of apprehension cross Marie's face. "It is more common to the north where the FARC and ELN, the nationalist guerrilla organisations, are very strong. They take people who they think are able to pay a big ransom, for the return of the captive: Businessmen, Gringo's who look rich, or representatives of foreign companies. Some are returned safely when the ransom is paid, a few are killed, but most are released after a while; it depends which faction capture them. The paramilitary is the most vicious. The Army, of course, kills some when they are trying to rescue them as well. Don't worry about it, you don't look rich enough!"

This was only partly reassuring, but we had come for the adventure. Joanne perhaps looked rather more affluent than the rest of us, although this was purely supposition as there had not been time to discover everybody's life histories; I made a mental note that I must try to get to know and understand her better. She was very pleasant, but just rather brash!

Carlos seemed to be a good source of information about all sorts of things; from the history of his country, to a very good knowledge of the fauna and flora. His appearance did not do justice to an extensive knowledge of his country and foreign news, but his job was leading parties such as ours with a very diverse lot of people. I was to discover over the next few days that he had in fact been to university in Bogota, but had opted for the rather more unconventional business of leading these tours, having got tired of the city life. He then brewed up "tinto", a strong black coffee drunk from small cups, and we shortly departed to our tents.

Whether it was the tinto or the day's events, it took me some while to drift off to sleep. My brain was going round with a mixture of thoughts, such as the kidnapping danger which was obviously why the Gonzales family lived behind guarded walls. This led on to wondering if my suspicions of the family having an involvement in the drugs trade was correct; they seemed to have accumulated wealth in quite a short time.

I could hear Colleen's gentle breathing from her sleeping bag next to me and this eventually soothed me to sleep as well.

Chapter 7

The next couple of days followed much the same pattern: a fairly early start, middle of the day siesta, and moving on early evening. The routine was interrupted by the odd stop to look at something of interest, or more usually to buy fresh fruit and veg at a village market. These were fascinating, as markets always are, wherever in the world. Some were just a few stalls set up in the street; others would be well organised with stalls selling every conceivable thing that could possibly be wanted in a household, from clothes through pots and pans to food of every description.

Carlos was a great asset, making sure we were not being fleeced and offering advice, such as, a better product could be got at a village a few miles further on. Colleen and I were quite restrained in our purchases as we knew we would have to carry whatever we bought for the rest of our travels, which were for an undetermined length of time. Joanne, on the other hand, seemed to be a compulsive buyer and enthused about each new market and stall she visited, loading herself up with all sorts of craft goods. Carlos encouraged us to do the buying of food, which caused a lot of amusement among the cheerful smiling locals.

We had by now crossed through the Cordillera to the east and were into the foothills again, with the Amazon basin stretching away for thousands of miles in front of us. The views were once again magnificent, disappearing into the haze. My imagination could picture the virgin forest stretching away for mile after mile, only broken by the occasional great river winding its course to the distant Atlantic. We turned in a north-easterly direction before stopping at the end of a long dirt track.

This was where the hard work started: carrying our packs and going on foot, but what we had really come for. The days were hot and humid now, after the clear air and cool nights of the mountains we had got used to after the first day. Now was the time to cut down and sort through our packs, as we had to carry everything from food through to a toothbrush. I could now see why Carlos was so stocky and strong: His pack was at least twice the size of any of the others. Marco and I felt we could cope with "yomping" a reasonable pack. Joanne had to be persuaded to cut down considerably, especially on things like makeup! Her many market purchases were left behind in the VW for our return; food and a water-bottle were much more important. The basics, like tents, were divided amongst us as fairly as possible. I think we all felt at this stage that our capabilities were rather more than they subsequently proved to be once we had been trekking for a few hours.

The plan was to cover a circular route which Carlos used often for his parties. We were all on a relaxed timetable, so we would be able to stop for longer at various points if they were of particular interest.

So the intrepid explorers set off into the jungle, knowing not what hidden dangers they would face!

After an hour of mostly downhill walking, carrying my probably 40 lb pack, I began to wonder why on earth we were doing this. It was very hot in amongst the trees, with no breath of a breeze to cool us, and plenty of insects buzzing around our heads and other exposed parts. The positive bit was that we were following a track, and there was a wonderful collection of birds and butterflies and flowers, which Carlos was excellent at pointing out for us and identifying. He was amazing at seeing things that we would never have noticed and would have just walked by. It was certainly nice to be out of the crowded minibus and into the quiet of the forest. We walked in single file and tended to get a bit strung out, chatting intermittently with whoever we were walking near; even Joanne was quieter than usual.

Periodically there would be sudden downpours of torrential rain, which might only last for a few minutes, or could be more prolonged for up to half an hour; they were mostly during the afternoon. Initially we rushed to find cover under a large tree, and frantically put on our waterproofs, but after repeating this several times and becoming just as hot and damp inside in the high humidity, I decided it was better not to bother; one seemed to dry off just as quickly when the sun came out again.

We stopped early that first day, as we all had aching muscles from the unaccustomed exercise. Carlos had chosen a clearing on the edge of a fast-flowing stream, where it tumbled down a succession of small waterfalls into dark pools edged with large boulders. Idyllic for soothing tired bodies. A real paradise, and I think we all felt that we would be happy to stay there and go no further.

We were not yet familiar enough with each other to dive in all together in the nude. Although it did not worry me, and Dom was game for anything, so it was agreed that the boys would go upstream to their own pool while the girls went a short way down to another pool. The water was surprisingly cold, but very invigorating, as the boys and I slipped in. It was rather like being in a Jacuzzi with the bubbling water from the waterfall, and delightfully refreshing after the heat of the day's walk.

Colleen and I were the duty cooks so I did not stay in for long. As I walked back from the pool there was a loud scream from the girls' direction, and a shout from Dom:

"Stay quite still, Marie."

I ran in the direction of all the noise, and on scrambling over a large rock found the four mermaids round their pool.

Colleen was nearly dressed, Dom still in the water; Joanne sitting on a rock the other side of the pool combing her hair, and little Marie on a rock, half turned towards me and staring down at the ground just below her feet, where she had obviously been just about to step.

"There's a snake just below her," Dom quietly informed me in an unflustered sensible voice.

Marie- Louise was visibly shaking with her wet hair hanging down to her shoulders, and quite unaware of the state of her thin "young boy-like" nakedness, not even bothering to cover herself with the towel clutched in her left hand beside her. Joanne jumped to her feet as I ran over towards Marie, but quickly reached for her towel as she saw me glance towards her. She was certainly a striking figure as she stood Amazon-like on the rock.

As I came up behind Marie I could see the greeny-coloured snake, coiled, and looking at her with beady unblinking eyes. It looked as if it would be about three feet long, thin with a pattern of red dots down the length of its back. This was the first snake we had seen since starting walking, but had all heard rustles in the leaves during the day.

I still had my towel in my hand and instinctively threw the towel so that it spread out over the snake's head (more from luck than any particular skill), at the same time grabbing Marie round the waist and unceremoniously dragging her backwards off the rock, which produced another loud scream. I assumed this to be from the surprise as she came out of her trance from looking at the snake, and probably being unaware of me coming up behind her. I quickly removed my shirt and offered it to Marie to hide her modesty before the rest of the gang arrived for a viewing; not that there was a lot to see as she was even thinner in the buff than she had appeared clothed.

The rest of the boys straggled in, led by Carlos looking like a gorilla, with his hairy body, as he tried to pull his shirt over his head. The other girls had had time to cover up decently so there was not too much embarrassment, except for Marie who by now was in floods of tears and rather shocked and clinging to Peter.

Meanwhile, Carlos walked over and picked up my towel to reveal the frightened snake.

"All OK. It's quite harmless. See, I can pick it up; it won't bite you, but it is always wise to be careful if you don't know." He then gave us a full description of its life cycle before gently releasing it.

"Are you alright Marie?" I asked.

"Yes, thank you for saving me, Cris. I just have a scraped bottom where you pulled me off the rock." She said seriously.

At which we all burst out laughing, with relief, except for Marie who could not see the funny side of it at first, but then joined in with us as she relaxed.

However it was an eye opener to us all of the hidden dangers there were in this, to us, unfamiliar country.

The following days passed quickly as we got into the routine of camp life and became hardened to the walking. Some days seemed to be nothing but scrambles up and down hills, but invariably it was eventually worth it when we came suddenly upon a wonderful panoramic view, or an ancient ruined village covered in vines and creepers, and quite unrecognisable until it was staring us in the face. Carlos continued to be a continual source of information and as a group we really got on very well, and had nothing as dramatic as the snake incident to upset us, other than the insects which came in all shapes and sizes. They could at times be an awful pest, biting or getting in one's eyes; but if we kept the repellent going it seemed to keep them at bay pretty well. Carlos, of course, seemed to be quite immune to them; at night we had mosquito nets to keep them out.

We had been out of touch now with other people for a week, other than one small village we had passed through without making contact with its shy inhabitants. I had completely lost my sense of direction but could only gather that we would get back to the minibus in four days. Should Carlos drop dead now, we would be completely lost. Colleen and I were really enjoying this life with no responsibility or worry of any kind and much appreciated the wonderful fauna and flora which was all around us constantly. Now we had got used to the strenuous exercise each day we both felt so fit and were able to really enjoy the surroundings. This part of the jungle was ever changing, be it the sudden glimpses of superb views, the constant chatter at certain times of the day of the teeming wildlife, or the wonderful sense of tranquillity and lack of bustle of the twenty-first century.

It, therefore, came as an unwelcome surprise, when early in the morning as the first rays of sunlight were creeping into our camp, that we were awakened by shouts. We sleepily poked our heads out of our tents to find ten swarthy unkempt men, armed to the teeth with a mixture of rifles, revolvers, submachine guns, rocket-launchers, and goodness knows what else, all draped in ammunition, and carrying large packs.

It didn't dawn on me immediately that these were rebel guerrillas, until I realised that Carlos was arguing violently with one of them. We stood huddled in a group unable to understand the heated exchange. His explanations were apparently not good enough, as suddenly the argument ended with him being struck on the side of the head with a rifle butt. He fell to he ground with what looked like a nasty wound beginning to pour blood down the side of his face. Dom ran forward bravely to assist him, only to have the rifle levelled at her menacingly by the leader who had struck Carlos to the ground.

These men were not playing, and it looked as if we were in real trouble.

43

Chapter 8

This was the worst scenario situation that we had all had in the back of our minds ever since the discussion about kidnapping, but had never imagined it could happen to us, after the reassurance from Carlos. Maybe I was reading too much into the situation and they were just out to steal from the rich gringos, not that we had anything of value between us that was worth stealing, other than cameras. If we were lucky they would take what they wanted and we would then be allowed to go on our way.

Carlos staggered back to his feet with blood running down the side of his head. Dom had not been put off by the rifle pointed at her and, much to the surprise of the man, had simply pushed the rifle to one side to get to Carlos's aid. She continued to support Carlos and staunch the bleeding, with her handkerchief. This was one plucky girl.

"Carlos. Are you all right?"

He gave no reply to this question. Whether it was because he was still confused from the severe blow, or just simply did not understand. He gave no indication. However, he was sufficiently compos mentus to give his attacker a pretty good verbal idea of what he thought of him.

While Carlos was venting his anger Dom had pulled dressings from her First Aid bag, which she always carried with her, and was mopping up his head and wrapping a bandage round the wound. He did now look rather funny with his mop of black hair sticking out of the top of the white bandage.

"Carlos, you look like a king with that crown on. Your wooden head can't have suffered though."

He glared at me without replying, but Dom made up for it.

"Cris, don't joke about it. He could have a serious injury and we are miles away from any hospital or medical help."

Carlos was recovering fast, and gently pushed Dom away with a gruff "thank you".

"These men are going to take you away to their camp," Carlos eventually was able to tell us once he had recovered sufficiently.

My worst fears seemed to have been correct. This was no hold-up. This sounded very like kidnapping.

We were now all out of our tents, but dressed in a rather motley assortment of clothes, and assembled in a tight group with Carlos and Dom at the front. The rebels had surrounded us and had lowered their weapons, but were just as threatening.

Marie was quietly sobbing as Peter held her tightly. Joanne for once seemed to be speechless, but had gone a pale shade of white. Colleen was next to me and had slipped her hand into mine. I gave it a squeeze to reassure her, though my heart was beating like mad inside. Marco, standing beside me, I could feel was tensed as if he could do something silly at any moment.

"Hold it, Marco, there are too many of them and too many guns pointing in our direction to try anything on at the moment. It would be a bloodbath if they start shooting," I whispered out of the corner of my mouth as I held his arm at the wrist to restrain him.

Colleen, on the other hand, outwardly appeared to be quite unfazed by the situation. Like Dom, another tough

45

cookie, the last thing we needed was hysterics. I felt really proud especially of them, but also of the whole group's reaction to this horrid situation we were in.

What were my thoughts? I am no tough cookie! but I am British and we put a brave face on things. Inside, apart from the increased heartbeat, I felt a mixture of anger, fear and excitement. We had come for adventure and this was it in big helpings.

While these thoughts were scampering through my head, Carlos had been talking again to the rebels; he now spoke to us:

"They want money: I have explained that you do not have any with you and, although tourists, you are not rich. So they have told me to go and get money from somewhere while you all stay with them. I am to make contact with them again at a place that they will tell me of later. Where I could go to get money I can't think, unless any of you have contacts. I hate to think what will happen if I can't get any."

"Who are these people?" I asked, trying to ignore the meaning of his last comment, and hoped the girls would not jump to any conclusions.

"I do not know; they will not say which group they belong to. I have never heard of kidnappers in this area, so they might be FARC or ELN, or just peasants, but I think that is unlikely as they are so well armed."

"Would you ask if they will let the girls go with you, and just leave us three here as the hostages." I indicated the other two men and myself.

This produced an immediate response simultaneously from Colleen and Dom, on the lines of "Not bloody likely, we are staying with you."

"Carlos, please ask them," I added as soon as I could get a word in.

At this request from Carlos, who it sounded made a very good case, a long discussion started amongst all ten members of the rebel group, with much waving of arms

46

and rapid talking. It seemed that they were split half-and-half as to it being a good or bad idea. The apparent leader eventually took control, calling for quiet, and pointing at Peter and Marie, said "You no come with us," with some sort of explanation to Carlos.

"He thinks that Peter and Marie look as if they will hold up his party; they look weak. They can come with me, but the rest of you must stay. I must apologise for letting this happen to you. Never before have I heard of any trouble down here. I am so ashamed that my countrymen should do this to you. I am just so angry....."

"Hold it, Carlos." I stopped his tirade in mid sentence. "We realise that this is no fault of yours. It is unfortunate to say the least, and not exactly what we had expected on this trip, but we must make the best of it and hope it can be resolved." This all sounded very restrained and was not at all what I was feeling inside.

In fact, Peter and Marie had been just as competent as the rest of us, since we took to our feet, after leaving the Volkswagen, but it was a good excuse to reduce the number of hostages. A discussion between us then started, with all of us trying to talk at the same time, just like the rebels had been. Peter, in particular, was reluctant to leave us behind, but gave in to our argument eventually, accepting that someone had to go with Marie-Louise and that the fewer hostages the better.

I, being the duty cook, brewed up coffee for us and included the rebels, as I felt we had to keep on good terms with them, and had to accept the situation we found ourselves in without upsetting our captors unnecessarily, though Marco was not of the same opinion.

I drew Carlos aside over our coffee.

"Carlos, will you please contact a Senor Frederiko Gonzales in Bogota for me and tell him what's happened. I think he may be in a position to help us." I was about to give him the address.

47

"You do mean the Senor Gonzales, who is a merchant in coffee and rubber?" he replied in a surprised voice, as he gave me a sideways look. "How do you know him, Cris?"

I explained that Colleen was his niece and that we had been staying with him. As I spoke his eyebrows went higher and higher and a look of incredulity spread over his face.

"Did you know that he is rumoured to be the head of a big drug ring?" He paused in deep thought before continuing. "We had better keep this to ourselves, I think. I am not sure how these pigs would react if they knew"

"Good Lord, I had no idea. Colleen had only just met him when we arrived out here." I went on to quickly explain the Gonzales family history.

I must admit this did not come as a complete surprise to me, thinking back to my thoughts and heated discussion with Colleen. If what Carlos said was true it could work either way for us to get our release.

Carlos was once again in deep discussion with the rebel leader, apparently arranging a rendezvous for the handover of the ransom money, if it was forthcoming, and subsequent return of us in exchange.

"I am to phone a mobile number in a week's time to contact them." Carlos informed me.

Our remaining food supplies we divided up so as to give Carlos, Peter, and Marie sufficient to get them back to some sort of civilisation. The rebels didn't appear to have equipment of any description other than their arms and ammunition, but perhaps their camp was not far away. I suspected that the little food we had left would have to be shared between us all.

So, with much embracing, hand-shaking and tears from Marie and Joanne, we parted company. They set off to travel back to the minibus as quickly as possible, while we set off in the opposite direction with the rebels to only they knew where, hoping that some sort of rescue would be stitched together to get us out of this jam.

Chapter 9

We all certainly felt the loss from the division of our little gang. The last few weeks had been a lot of laughs and we had all bonded really very well. The odd spat had been short-lived and trivial, and soon resolved by changing walking partners, or going off on one's own; there was certainly plenty of space to do it in. I would particularly miss Carlos. He had looked after us in all respects admirably and was a very interesting and knowledgeable travelling companion. I just hoped that his knock on the head was nothing serious. It would be awful for Peter and Marie if he suddenly collapsed or something. They would be totally lost, short of food and with a sick man on their hands; neither of them were the most practical of people.

Ten minutes after we set off, Marco, who was walking just behind me, suddenly blurted out: "Do you think Carlos knew that we were going to be kidnapped and was in on the whole thing?" This certainly came as a surprise to me as it had never crossed my mind. I had sensed at the time that he was particularly upset, but had thought it a reaction to the situation rather than feeling that Carlos was involved.

"No, not possibly," I answered crossly. "How could he have known where we would be at this time? It's not as if there are

49

any landmarks to be able to tell them where we would be. I think you are being very disloyal to even consider it."

"He could have arranged it before we left and told them the route we would be following. Maybe they have been tracking us for several days, or he has left signs behind. It's all possible."

"How do you account for the rifle butt to his head then. It was no pretend blow, I could see that from the wound it left, and could have done more damage than is apparent; he could have a fracture of the skull for all I can tell." said Dom joining in the argument, walking behind Marco.

We left it at that, but I could feel that Marco was still brooding on it. On the other hand it did seem strange that the rebels had found us in this vast forest; but I suppose we were on a route that Carlos used with other parties and, although the population was pretty sparse, there was I am sure local gossip of a sort. Also there were not that many routes we could have been taking. Anyway, speculation at this stage was not going to change the situation one bit.

Personally, I needed all my attention to be on the march. The rebels were setting a pretty stiff pace, quite different to the amble that we had been doing previously and had got used to. Also, the track, was through much thicker bush and we had to keep a good look out not to trip over tree roots or get caught by hanging vines.

We were travelling in single file, which was all this path would allow. The rebels were both in front and behind, with two of them in the middle of the column. So there was no hope of escape, which anyway would be pretty foolish as we had no idea of where we were and very little indication of which direction we were going.

It got gradually tougher, with more steep ups and downs and without a pause to recover our breath. After three hours non-stop I could see that the girls were beginning to tire and needed a rest. Colleen, with her limited understanding of the language, was able to make this known to the leader who indicated that in half an hour we would get there, wherever "there" was. He did, however, tell three of his men to carry the girls' rucksacks.

Over an hour later we suddenly walked into a small clearing beside a stream. There were five small khaki-coloured tents under the trees and a shelter of branches and leaves which looked as if it was where they cooked, though no sign of a fire burning.

The leader indicated that this was where we would stop, and we all sank to the ground thoroughly exhausted.

We put up our tents (directed to be under the trees rather than in the open which we would have normally done.) and had a wash in the stream; this was under the supervision of two guards. One of the rebels got the fire going and started to produce a meal. We had not eaten, other than snacks of chocolate, all day so accepted the stew of beans, and God knows what else, readily.

We decided, after some dissent by Marco and Joanne, that it would be best to pool our food with theirs, except for the few snacks we had left. I felt if we did not they would probably commandeer it anyway. It was better that we should try and build up a relationship of some sort with them. At least then if the worst happened (they decided to kill us.) it might make them think twice about it. Their supplies must be very limited, and we wondered from where they would renew them. Not a lot of supermarkets in this neck of the woods!

Sitting round the fire, after the meal, sipping at our scalding mugs of tinto, very dilute to what we were used to, we got into conversation with them.

Somewhat hesitantly we gathered from them that they were of the ELN faction, one of the Marxist guerrilla movements and did not usually operate in this area, but were here to see what support there was from the locals for the movement. They had heard from the villagers that there was a tourist group trekking through the area, so decided to boost their funds by kidnapping us.

This put paid to Marco's theory that Carlos had been in on the plot. Although by the continuing sullen look on his face he was still not completely convinced.

The leader was called Julio Cesar and his second in command was Yolande Flores.

"That's a girl's name, surely?" asked Colleen in surprise.

Yolande at this undid the bandanna she had been wearing all day round her head and revealed her short cropped hair. She did now indeed look female whereas before I had assumed she was a young boy. Somehow, without the bandanna one noticed that she was not completely flat chested.

"Are there many girls active in your movement?"

"Yes, but most are not fighting in the field. I like the life and believe in the cause and want to be with Julio who is my husband." This came as another surprise as they had shown no signs of affection for one another, but perhaps we had just not been on the right wavelength.

She was a tough wiry-looking girl of average height and had kept going all day, apparently, just as easily as the men of the group and carrying an equally large pack and assortment of weapons.

We were all more than ready to get to sleep that night, but first Julio insisted that we leave our boots inside their tents to prevent us trying to escape during the night. This precaution was not necessary as we were all far too exhausted to contemplate escaping and wouldn't know where to go anyway.

The next week passed slowly, following mostly the same routine: Early morning start from the overnight camp after a mug of coffee; continuous hiking until mid-afternoon, always at the same ferocious pace as the first day, and then set up camp again. One of the rebels would then cook a meal of sorts and we would be early into our sleeping bags, completely exhausted.

I noticed that during the day often one of the men would disappear for a couple of hours, and on return sometimes arrived back with a scrawny chicken or such-like to supplement our meagre food supplies. They obviously had a good knowledge of the area in spite of apparently not being locals. Otherwise, we would harvest berries or fruit if we found them.

On one afternoon the man on point position came upon a small unsuspecting wild pig and was able to catch hold of it before cutting its throat. This gave us a good feast that evening, but did not go far between fifteen of us.

The group were very reluctant to make any unnecessary noise and definitely loath to use their rifles to shoot any game such as deer which we occasionally saw. I asked Yolande about this one evening as we sat round the fire.

"We do not have unlimited ammunition. We never know when we will get into a fire fight with the Government forces, or the paramilitary pigs, and need every bit we have," she told me vehemently, and spat into the fire in disgust. "Also sound travels a long way in the forest and we don't want to advertise where we are."

"It is quite likely that your friends have reached the police and a search has started for you, or we may meet with soldiers looking for coca fields."

It was a very gruelling routine that we were being forced to follow. The five of us had lost a lot of weight due to the continual moving on with no rest days and the strenuous exercise and poor diet we were surviving on. I was not sure how long Joanne, in particular, would be able to keep up the punishing pace. She was a big girl, but although like the rest of us had become much fitter, she was definitely suffering more than Colleen and Dom. We had all cut our packs down to the minimum; often the articles we discarded were picked up by one of the rebels.

We had some interesting talks round the fire in the evenings. Yolande had a smattering of passable English and

53

Julio was understandable with help from Colleen or Marco. They all believed passionately in their cause and had a great hatred of the ruling class, the rich in particular. Their backgrounds were from middle-class families rather than from the very poor peasant class. Politics seemed to be at the heart of everything, and the Catholic Church played a big part as well. I really found the group a likeable crowd whom I would have had a lot of sympathy with if our circumstances had been different.

We lost track of time, but I think it was on the ninth or tenth day that Julio heard from Carlos, although we were given no indication whether he had somehow come up with money or any solution to our captivity.

They were to meet at the town of Neiva, which was within two days' walk of us, but this could mean anything as they seemed to have no sense of distance.

The same day we heard several helicopters or low-flying planes passing nearby, but apparently unable to see us through the thick tree canopy. It did, however, disturb Julio and the others who were of the opinion that they were searching for us, as there was no reason for aircraft in this area. It could be the American led operation to find and destroy the coca fields.

Julio became much more alert. We no longer had a hot meal each evening, as he was afraid of the smoke from the fire being seen or smelt. The smell of wood smoke travels a long way down wind. We didn't put up tents at night and slept with our boots on ready for a quick get away. Our improved relationship with them had lead to a certain degree of trust from them as I had hoped. All this only increased our growing fatigue and I am sure we all prayed silently that we would soon be released.

Chapter 10

These all proved to be good precautions as, at daybreak on the second day after we first heard the aircraft, we were woken by several shots, followed by silence. The half light and heavy mist made it confusing from which direction the shots had come.

Julio and his gang obviously had a well-rehearsed plan of action. Immediately they were struggling into their packs, grabbing weapons, and disappearing into the forest. It would seem that the shots had come from the rebel sentry on duty down the track from the direction we had come yesterday evening.

We all sat up at the first disturbance, just as alert as the group. We just had time to grab our packs, as Yolande shouted at us and marshalled us into the undergrowth, waving her Kalashnikov at us to hurry. The rest of the gang quickly melted into the trees in the opposite direction.

Very soon there was a resumption of the firing, intensifying rapidly, as what sounded like a light machine gun opened up firing short bursts.

I could hear bullets whispering through the leaves, and thumps as they struck the trees, and the dew or moisture from the mist cascaded round us.

During army training I had run under live firing, but this

was quite different. These bullets were being fired in anger and meant to kill. The adrenaline was flowing fast through my veins and no doubt the others felt the same. I had no idea what their thoughts might be. This was a situation that perhaps we had not wished to think of beforehand and had certainly never expected. The only plus factor was that there was no time to really think, and the rush of adrenaline round our bodies gave us extra strength to get as far away as possible as quickly as we could.

We ran as low as we could following a game trail in the direction away from the firing; there were several louder explosions, which I recognised as grenades from my army training, and then silence. The whole fight seemed to be over within five minutes of the first shot; we had no idea of the outcome, but kept going urged on by Yolande's commands and directions. It passed rapidly through my mind that this might be a good moment to escape, but then I instantly realised that with both sides on heightened alert they would probably all shoot at the slightest movement; not a good idea.

We continued like this for what seemed an eternity, but when I glanced at my watch it was only twenty minutes further on. We were all puffing fit to bust and dripping with sweat at this sudden exertion, when Yolande signalled us to stop and lie down in thick bush and keep silent; not easy with our laboured breathing.

We lay like sardines snuggled up together in a row, with Marco and me at each end and the girls in the middle; our packs pushed in front to perhaps give some protection. Yolande was about three yards ahead with her gun held ready to fire from the prone position. I could feel Colleen next to me shivering with the reaction from the run and the 'excitement', and I was probably reacting in the same way.

I had time now to realise what a dangerous situation we were in, before I had assumed the rebels would do an exchange of us for money, or whatever it was that they wanted. In fact, we were the pawns in the middle that the government forces, if that was who had been firing, were trying to get back without giving anything, and we could easily have been or might be killed in the process. This could go on for ages with us being chased all over the forest becoming more tired and weaker each day.

I could see Yolande tense in front of me and raise her Kalashnikov, and at the same moment heard the murmur of voices not far away in the direction we had come from. I prayed that, if it was the "enemy", Yolande would have the sense not to open fire on them, as we being so close to her would be bound to be hit badly too. I had no faith in this theory knowing what a fanatic she was who would not give up without a fight to the death. Probably a wise policy if half the stories we had been told were correct about the opposition.

I put my arm round Colleen who was next to me and pulled her gently towards me, not that I was able to give her much protection, but it was a reassurance for both of us.

It sounded as if we were lying not ten yards back from a track, which was where their voices were coming from as they approached. Yolande could see more than I could, as she was able to recognise the gang as they passed in front of our hiding place, and she gave a bird call I had heard them use before. It was sufficient to stop them and she rose carefully to her feet. Everybody was naturally pretty twitchy after the close encounter. We stayed firmly where we were, much safer lying flat on the ground and I was glad of the extra rest.

It made me realise how easy it would be to stage an ambush by just lying in wait beside a track. It was lucky that whoever the opposition were, they had apparently got caught in this way rather than us.

"Dom, please come and see Miquel quickly," Julio said in a loud whisper, but with urgency in his voice.

She was on her feet in an instant and pushing past Yolande to the track. I followed close behind and saw that two of the rebels were just lowering the young Miquel to the ground. He had been shot in the upper chest on the right side; his shirt was covered in blood and he had blood round his mouth; he sounded as if he was having difficulty in breathing; it looked as if he had probably taken the bullet in the lung. I could not see his back to check if the bullet had exited there; if it had there probably would be a lot of damage. He was just conscious, but in a lot of pain. It did not look good for him.

"What have you got in the way of field dressings?" Dom asked as she cut away Miquel's shirt with her knife. She was immediately the professional nurse, absorbed in the casualty and quite oblivious to her surroundings and the dangerous situation we were in. She had changed from the jolly hostage to the dedicated carer in a flash: Totally in control of the situation, unflustered, and clearing the bits of shirt and grass away with deft fingers.

Julio handed over a small pack and I tipped the contents out onto the ground. Not very much by the standards I had been used to in the army, and to Dom it must have seemed very inadequate. There were however field dressings, bandages, gauze and a small bottle of what I took to be some sort of antiseptic.

"What is this, Julio?" I asked, holding up the bottle.

"For cleaning wounds." So I was right.

"Give me some water in a mug so I can clean him up a bit and we can then see what the damage is." Dom was quite calm, as I would have expected from her. Her movements were quick, but gentle, and between us we soon had a dressing bandaged firmly over the wound, and as we had sat him partially up I could see that there was no exit wound.

"The bullet is still in there then. Is that a good thing or bad?" I asked Dom.

"Good, that he only has the one wound, but it will have to be got out pretty quickly. Anyway, he will need to be seen by a doctor as soon as possible. I have no idea what damage he has inside his chest. The shock of the injury is considerable and I have nothing other than Paracetamol as a pain killer."

Turning to Colleen, the others had followed me and were all gathered round where we knelt on the ground. I passed on this information.

"Will you make sure that Julio understands the situation, and we must get to a doctor a.s.a.p. We are also going to need some sort of stretcher to carry him on," I said quickly.

Thank goodness for Colleen's grasp of Spanish, which had improved in the local dialect over the last few weeks. She also asked him what had become of the attacking force as it seemed to me we were rather vulnerable, all standing in a huddle in the middle of the track with, as far as I could see, none of the rebels on guard. They had all been rather rattled by the encounter, and being mostly only youngsters this was probably the first time they had ever been in a fire fight.

On Julio's order two of them went back down the track for a recce to see where the army, if that's who it was, had got to, while two more set about cutting branches with their machetes to make a stretcher. The others did take up defensive positions round where Dom and I were working over Miquel. They were therefore not completely "green". Marco, I instructed to get Colleen and Joanne back into the cover off the track.

"We are only about five hours' walk from the nearest village and road and an hour's drive into Neiva," Colleen ascertained. "Though I would double those times as their judgement of time is not the best, and there is Miquel to carry."

Chapter 11

This was going to be a hard slog for the rebels, to carry Miquel out and to give us all some cover from another attack. I decided that it would be to our advantage to continue our policy of being as helpful as possible. One of the recce party who had gone back down the track, returned to say that there was no sign of the opposition, which was quite a relief. If it hadn't been for the gunfire and Miquel's severe wound I would have felt that nothing had changed from an hour ago. The forest had not altered, the peace of the place was the same (if you can call the constant bird, insect, and monkey noise peace!), we were all here and feeling just as exhausted.

I was rather concerned about the lack of command and organisation of the party; I had the impression that this was the first encounter that the group had had with the opposition, and their training, if they ever had any, had neglected to cover a situation such as this. Their reactions should have been instantaneous; Julio should have taken command, rather than the grabbing of packs and panicky dash in the direction of the firing. This was I suppose a credit to them that they hadn't all just scattered in different directions like a lot of rabbits. Yolande had reacted well, marshalling us away from the overnight campsite while still getting us to a place that she felt would be a rendezvous.

As we prepared Miquel for evacuation and reallocated the packs, I asked Julio, "What happened back there, you were rather surprised were you not?"

"Yes, in a way we were. You are right Cris; Miquel was the sentry I had posted to watch the track we came on yesterday. I don't know whether he was asleep or they crept up on him without him hearing them until the last moment, it was only just light and misty, but as you can see he got himself shot. He did manage to get a shot at them as well, so was not totally taken by surprise. A patrol of five must have been dropped from a helicopter to search for you. We definitely hit one if not more of them in the fire fight and it would seem that they have pulled back, but of course they now know where we are and probably can guess that you are with us."

This was an honest answer at least. It did not fill me with much faith for the rest of the day, however. If Julio was correct they could be coming for us again once they had regrouped.

At the first opportunity I got Marco and the girls together and explained the situation as Julio had told me.

"The question is, now we know that the army is on our tail, do we try and make a break for it, and hope that we can make contact with them again, without getting shot or lost. or do we hang on with Julio and the gang and hope to be released as planned; or try and escape when we are nearer to Neiva?"

Dom was quite definite when she replied, "I plan to stay and do what I can for Miquel until they get him to a doctor. He's in a bad way and I can't do much for him as there is no morphine to relieve the pain but I can try and make him as comfortable as possible."

"Joanne, what do you feel we should do?"

"I don't really know. Part of me says I've had enough of this trekking and unpleasantness and I just want to get out of here as soon as possible and have a hot bath, but if we did go now, anything could happen and it might be better

61

to wait. There's also the question of not knowing where on earth we are. Quite important."

"Marco, what about you?"

As I thought he would, he was all for making a break now and taking a chance. I had realised ever since the kidnap that he would rather have got away right at the beginning.

"Colleen, I will stick with you. What's your feeling?"

She smiled at me, "I rather hoped you might, but you are passing the buck! I want to stay with Dom and see what turns up later on."

"OK. I think the general feeling is that we stay for the time being. Marco, are you prepared to go along with that for the present? I think it is important that we stick together. All I ask is please let us know if you suddenly plan to disappear."

By this time Miquel had been loaded on to the make-do stretcher. They had made it up of two stout branches with long vines tied and wound between them, with another branch crossways at each end to hold it all apart. Blankets had been spread on this and Miquel laid on top. It was not going to be very comfortable for him and a hell of a weight to carry. He wasn't a big lad, in fact rather skinny, but it would be an awkward 65 or so kilos to negotiate.

"Julio, let's get this show on the road." There seemed to be too much 'Manyana' about them and no sense of urgency to get Miquel repaired, or to move on from so near where the action had taken place. I could see that a few orders from a sergeant of the British Army, even if I had had my stripes removed and was only an RASC driver, were required. I'm not sure that they really realised how seriously wounded Miquel was.

"Julio, you must have one man out on point ahead of us, and one bringing up the rear to protect us from behind; four to carry the stretcher and the other three will have to have double packs but discard as much as possible. Marco and I can carry the remaining food and some other essentials. We will stop for ten minutes each hour and you can swap the stretcher carriers with the others."

He seemed to be quite happy that I should take charge in this way. The division of the labour was not really very satisfactory as it would be very energy-draining carrying the stretcher. We might well find that an hour was too long for each stint.

The five hours to the village turned out to take us eight, and were not pleasant. We all had the extra weight to carry and the stretcher was difficult to handle on the narrow track, added to which we were crossing an area of steep-sided valleys, densely wooded, and the track was very muddy and slippery. Concealed roots of trees hidden in the mud or leaf mould were a constant problem for the stretcher bearers. Consequently, Miquel had a pretty rough ride; being dropped several times and slid up or down the worst parts where it became so steep it was just a scramble. We all, including the girls, had to lend a hand at times. Thankfully he had lapsed into unconsciousness after about six hours and I could see that Dom was really worried about him.

The ground levelled out a bit and at last we came to the edge of the forest with cultivated ground in front of us. Julio called a halt as we caught up with the man on point. We all fell exhausted to the ground without even taking off our packs. Needless to say Dom was fussing round Miquel like a mother hen, wiping his brow with a wet cloth and renewing his dressing with our meagre supply of pads and bandage. He briefly regained consciousness and with a faint smile murmured something unintelligible before sinking away again, hopefully, into pain-free oblivion.

"We will stop here and Yolande will go into the village to find some transport to take us to Neiva. I am sure there will not be a doctor here."

At this comment Dom looked up sharply but did not say anything.

"Julio, we really must get Miquel treated as soon as possible. I don't think you realise how serious this is."

I was only putting into words what Dom's look had implied to me.

"You think I don't care." Julio replied heatedly before turning abruptly away.

I got the impression that Julio was not quite so keen on the idea of exchanging us for a ransom and would rather just melt away unnoticed. There had been some fairly heated exchanges between him and the other gang members since the fight. They looked as if they were perhaps not so committed to the cause and had lost their bottle somewhat. I think our kidnap could have been more of a spur of the moment thing, which they were perhaps beginning to regret.

Yolande returned after two hours. She had persuaded someone with a pick-up truck to take us into Neiva. I don't know how she achieved this as she had no money and naturally had not taken any weapon with her. There was only room for Miquel, the five of us, Julio and Yolande. The rest of the gang would make their own way to an agreed meeting place. The good news was that she had spoken to Carlos on the phone, who would be at Neiva to meet us, but she had no idea what arrangements had been made for us other than he had said everything was arranged. I think we had all reached the stage where we really couldn't care less whether there would be a pot of gold waiting for the exchange or we were lined up against a wall.

We squashed into and onto the very ramshackle old Peugeot truck; Joanne and Julio with the driver in the front; Miquel, now off the stretcher, lying on the floor bed at the back, with the rest of us sitting on the sides round him. I had my doubts whether the truck was up to this sort of weight and would be able to cope with any steep hills.

I wasn't far wrong, but an hour's drive of grinding gears and clouds of foul exhaust fumes brought us to the outskirts of Neiva.

We stopped outside a wood and corrugated-iron house in a real slum area of the town, and unloaded Miquel inside. He was looking very white, with shallow breathing, sweating profusely, obviously with a high temperature; and to my eye looked as if he was going to have a job to make it. Dom had worked hard doing what she could for him, which was not much more than trying to keep him on the stretcher and wiping the sweat from his face. She looked absolutely out on her feet. She had been a constant tower of strength since the ambush. Apart from her continuous care of Miquel she had encouraged and goaded the stretcher carriers to keep going on the most tricky sections and had been an inspiration to us all. Looking round the party, the exhaustion applied to everybody.

Yolande disappeared again to find Carlos. She returned twenty minutes later in a large black expensive-looking car and, much to my surprise, not only did Carlos emerge but none other than Fredericko Gonzales.

This was certainly putting the cat amongst the pigeons.

When I had told Carlos to contact Fredericko, I had never expected that he would actually turn up in person. I had been more concerned that someone should know what had become of us, and possibly arrange some means of getting us out of this situation.

Chapter 12

"My little Colleen: Are you all right? Have these pigs hurt you in any way?"

Colleen was quite unable to answer any of these questions as she was enveloped in one of Fredericko's enormous bear hugs and was just as surprised as I was to see her uncle. I had not told her that I had asked Carlos to contact him.

Next it was my turn, but without the hug.

"Cris, why did you let my little niece be treated like this?"

Without waiting for an answer he turned to Julio, never mind that I had had the same treatment as Colleen. It was obviously all my fault for getting her into that situation.

"Have you any idea what you have done? Do you know who I am, and do you realise what an insult you have done to my family? This is my niece, my own flesh and blood."

This is just the gist of what was said, as it sounded as if it was well embroidered with every insult and foul description of Julio's family that one could possibly think of. I could imagine that it came from the school of life where Fredericko's upbringing had first started. It did not match with the suave Fredericko that I had got to know while we stayed with him in Bogota, though he was still impeccably dressed even to the buttonhole in his well cut suit.

The penny had dropped with Julio, with a little help of whispered asides from Carlos. His face had become ashen as he looked from Fredericko to Colleen. He had really jumped from the frying pan of the army into the fire of Fredericko and his organisation, and I could make a good guess that he would rather be in the fire at this moment. I could see that my earlier guess that he was rather regretting the whole operation was certainly now true.

"Senor, I meant no harm. I had no idea that Colleen was your esteemed niece. I would not have taken her if I had known." he wheedled and stammered. Quite unlike the laid back Julio we had come to know over the days since our capture.

I stepped forward to stop the flow of invective that I guessed was about to start again. Not so much to save Julio from a richly deserved bollocking, but we had to move on and get Dom's patient proper medical care.

"Fredericko, what can we do for this wounded man? He needs attention immediately or he may well die."

"So what, he is just another of the pigs that kidnapped you. Why should I care what happens to him."

"Uncle Fredericko, they have not harmed us. We have just had a big adventure and now you have come to save us." Colleen said, as she took his arm with a close embrace.

I hoped she was not laying it on too thickly. He was no fool. She now went into petulant mode with a downcast face and pout.

"You must help this poor man, or Cris and I will return to England and not speak to you again."

"Who do you think I am that I can help this criminal. The President to give him a pardon, or the United Nations?"

The whole thing was like some comic opera or theatre farce. If we had not been the actual characters involved one could have stood back and had a jolly good laugh. It was really all to do with the loss of face by Fredericko, but he would never have admitted it.

Colleen went back next to the buttering-up mode. I think Fredericko could see exactly what was being done to him and was playing along with the game. Colleen could also see that he knew, but still persisted. She was a devious little minx!

"Please Uncle, just for me your little niece who you have only just met. I know you are a very important man in Colombia.".

"OK, OK, you win." He said with a wide smile.

I could see a look of relief cross Dom's face. I think she was too exhausted to have realised the "play" going on between the two of them.

He turned to Carlos and gave him instructions where to take Miquel, and to say that Senor Gonzales had ordered that this pig should be given every chance to make a full recovery.

We immediately started to move Miquel back into the pickup.

"I suppose you wish me to let these two criminals go free as well?"

He gestured towards Julio and Yolande.

"But of course dear uncle!" Colleen replied with a sweet smile.

He turned to Julio and Yolande with the sort of look that would crack a Brazil nut.

"Don't ever cross my path again. I have an excellent memory and never forget a face. Go back to the hole you came out of and make sure your colleagues keep out of my way in future."

So this was to be how our adventure came to an end. We would all go away and live happily ever after, just like a pantomime fairy tale! I was pleased at the result, in spite of the ordeal that we had been put through. We all shook hands with Julio and Yolande, much to the disgust of Fredericko; not exactly saying thank you for the trip, but it had been an experience. We said a special thank-you to Carlos for looking after us so well. He had been a tower of strength and was someone I would really like to meet up with again. He told us that Peter and Marie-Louise had decided that they had had enough of travel adventures, and returned to Germany apparently to begin a happily married life in their dull routine jobs.

Dom reluctantly gave up her patient with strict instructions to Carlos to tell the doctor how Miquel should be treated, and we five then squashed into Fredericko's car for the journey back to Bogota.

I think we all slept most of the way. It had been a very long and exhausting day since we were rudely awakened by the first shots, and it was now late in the evening, and early morning before we drew up at the Gonzales house.

In spite of the hour the whole household was on the steps to meet us, Fredericko having phoned ahead from the car to let them know that we were safe. Mama immediately ushered away the three girls to their rooms, while Marco and I refused stiff drinks and asked to be allowed to take hot baths before making up our sleep deficit.

"Fredericko, may we please talk tomorrow to hear how you became involved." I was also, with my enquiring mind, keen to know more about the Gonzales family and their business.

Much brighter, but not so early, we all met up over lunch out on the terrace in the shade of large umbrellas. Looking around our party I decided we had fared really quite well; we had all lost a lot of weight and were deeply tanned. Joanne had probably suffered most; she looked slightly haggard which her make up was not able to completely hide; in my opinion she looked much better without make-up as we had got to see her on the trek. Dom looked typically outback Ossie, as if she could go through the whole experience again starting today. Colleen, after a good night's sleep had a healthy glow to her face; I had a good companion in her to tackle the next part of our trip, whatever it might be. As for Marco and myself, we were leaner and fitter and perhaps even a little wiser.

We had undoubtedly been lucky to have the contact with the Gonzales family and not to have sustained any injuries, either gunshot or broken limbs. We had crossed some pretty rough territory with a lot of natural hazards.

The other three decided after lunch that it was time to move on and not to abuse the Gonzales hospitality any longer. Marco and Joanne had agreed to travel together for a while and were headed for Mexico, while Dom, ever the loner, was off to Peru or Chile to find a nursing job to raise funds for further travel. After much hugging and kissing and promises to keep in touch, they departed during the afternoon.

Colleen and I needed to get together to make our plans, but first I wanted to hear from Fredericko about his part in the kidnap and if he would tell me what position he really held in the Colombian hierarchy.

Later that evening over long cooling drinks the three of us started talking.

"Fredericko, have you any suggestions where we should travel on to? We have made use of your generosity for long enough. Not to mention the hassle of getting ourselves kidnapped."

"Oh, that was nothing. I could not lose my new found niece."

"Well it was a bit more than nothing to us, Uncle. Thank you very much for your help." Colleen said with a broad smile and reaching out to squeeze his forearm.

"Well, it depends what you want to see." Fredericko hurried on, obviously touched by Colleen's gesture. "You obviously enjoy the wide outdoors, so why not go south to the spectacular mountains and deserts of Chile, or go north to the rain forest of Mexico in the Yucatan. If you go in that direction you can travel on up the west coast of America and Canada and into the empty wide open spaces of the Yukon and Alaska, which I am told are wonderful if you enjoy unpopulated space. You will find all are safer than Colombia."

"Talking of being safe," Colleen said, "We have not really thanked you for coming to our rescue. I can't think what would have happened to us if you had not."

"I would second that." I added. "Please tell us your side of the story."

"There's not a lot to tell. I had already heard that you had been kidnapped from Rogero, who should never have allowed you to go on such a trip, and other sources I have. I had people start to make enquiries and then had the phone call from Carlos, and you really know the rest."

"Did you not tell the army, as they seemed to be looking for us, and as you know caught up with us."

"No I did not tell the army. I am not exactly friendly with them. The fight your people had with them was just a patrol looking for coca that happened to stumble across you. I do have a contact in the control headquarters so was able to make sure they did not follow you. My people were much more likely to get you out safely."

"Uncle you seem to have a lot of influence in Colombia and a lot of contacts with many strange people. Are you in the cocaine business? Because that is what we were told."

Now it was out and that was a direct question which he would have a job not to answer. Colleen, I had felt, had been brooding on this ever since I had first implied it to her. I wondered how much he would divulge to us. I was anyway glad that she had asked the question rather than me.

"You have been talking to too many people who have told you all sorts of things. You are family so I suppose have a right to know how I have managed to get to this position and the standard of living which we enjoy. I take it your father has told you nothing about our childhood?"

71

"Your grandparents were poor and we lived in an area of a lot of crime in a small two-roomed house. We both went to school until we were twelve so we learnt to read and write. Your father was always keen to get on and improve himself through learning, whereas I was in too much of a hurry to get away from our neighbourhood and got in with the crime gangs. This was why your father left Colombia to get away from me and my associates; he was not proud of his younger brother and didn't wish to get involved with *scams*.

"I prospered through crime, though I am not particularly proud of things I got involved with at that time, and only I know what those things were, and that's how it will remain, although I suppose I would not be where I am today if things had been different. But who knows. More recently, you have guessed correctly; we have been very involved in the buying of coca and the manufacturing and export of cocaine, principally to the States. As you know we also trade in less controversial products like coffee, rubber and the craft products.

Now, there you are, you know all about your wicked uncle. I expect now you will want to leave, as you are ashamed of me and what I do. It is not surprising that your father has never wanted to tell you about me. I would like to meet him again before we get too old, but he would never want to forgive me. We are too different and set in our ways and lifestyles now."

Colleen had been very attentive while she learnt the family history. She made no reply to the admission of the question of the cocaine.

"Have you never been in touch with my father in all these years?"

"No, we have not spoken in all that time, but I have in the last few years had my people make discreet enquires about the family and what you were all doing. I know all about you, Colleen, where you live and what you do.

"I can't say I approve, but I can see that you have the

72

Gonzales desire to improve yourself by making money and since meeting you here I can tell that you are a credit to the family. We will not discuss the matter again and no one other than us three will ever know. I would ask that you consider very carefully giving up your profession. If you need money you have only to ask me."

Colleen had blushed deeply at learning that the secret was out. Her questioning of her uncle was not meant to have disclosed her past life and she obviously felt deeply embarrassed.

"I am sorry Uncle, I would rather that you had not known, but thank you for being so understanding. You now know what your wicked niece has been doing. I would be eternally grateful if you never tell my parents. So would you like me to leave, or are we now all square?" she said with a cheeky smile that nobody would have been able to resist.

"Don't push your luck too far, young lady!"

Fredericko turned to me: "Since you arrived here I also have found out all about you, Cris. I needed to know that you were good enough for my Colleen. In spite of your sometimes chequered past I believe you are a resourceful and kind man. In some ways very like myself as a young man."

I was beginning to like Fredericko more and more as I got to know him. I was glad I had passed his test as a suitable companion to Colleen as I would hate to get on the wrong side of him.

We all had things to hide, so we changed the subject of discussion of the family failings to more general subjects, and shortly afterwards were called in to supper by Mama. I did wonder how much Fredericko discussed with Mama about his business and other things. Not a lot I think, but she was a very astute woman and not very much happened in that household that she did not know all about.

Later, as I lay wakeful under the mosquito net, unused to sleeping on a comfortable bed, my mind was going round and round sorting out all the new information I had gleaned. The inkling of an idea started to form.

No, it would be idiotic.

Fredericko would never agree.

The consequences were too great. I could not ask Colleen to be party to such a daft idea.

Think of the excitement.

We could make a lot of money.

It would be a great adventure.

No, I am getting too old for that sort of thing.

It would be breaking the laws of every country.

Oh what the hell, I can put the idea to Colleen and see what she thinks.

At which point I drifted off to a deep dreamless sleep.

Chapter 13

The next morning, as I lay half awake, I still could not get last night's thoughts out of my head; once again they were going round and round. Pros and cons; this and that; every little argument for and against.

Come on, this is quite stupid; make a decision, otherwise it will just continue to bother you, I said to myself.

Fredericko returned from his office at midday and I managed to catch him alone in his study.

"May I come in and have a chat to you about a proposition that's been forming in my mind? You may well tell me not to be a bloody fool, or not to get involved in such a potentially dangerous venture, especially as I would only do it if Colleen was in agreement, with which you might disapprove. It also involves you."

This was not my usual direct approach to things. I was much more likely to open my big mouth and say what I felt without thinking.

"Well, what is it? Stop hesitating, Cris, I won't bite your head off."

"OK, here goes then: What if I bought some cocaine from you to smuggle into England? I am not meaning just a small amount for my own use, not that I use it or have any

75

desire to, but several kilos, as a business proposition to make some money."

Fredericko's reaction was not what I had feared. He even seemed mildly interested and not particularly surprised, as he smiled broadly and chuckled quietly.

"Firstly, have you mentioned this to Colleen?"

"No, I only thought of it last night after we had our talk, and I am not even sure that I want to take the risk of being caught and spending another spell in prison. I did not enjoy the last experience as a guest of the army. Cocaine smuggling would mean quite a long spell inside, not to mention all the other aspects of it." I had just stopped myself in time from saying that it might be ruining the lives of masses of people. That would have been rather tactless in view of Fredericko's trade.

"Have you thought at all how you would do it?"

"No, there would have to be a lot of planning, and I would need to have your help in getting the cocaine here in the first place."

"I know that I do it and have made a lot of money from it, but I am not involved in the actual smuggling and distribution in other countries. We'll have a talk to Colleen first and see what she thinks, though I am not that keen to have her involved in a venture of this sort."

After lunch Colleen and I went to lie in the sun on the loungers round the swimming pool to talk about our plans, though I found her rather too distracting lying there in the briefest of brief bikinis which was finding it difficult to keep all of her adequately hidden.

I was getting cold feet again about mentioning cocaine to her and had decided there were other ways of making money that would involve less risk or worry, and I did not really need the money anyway.

"OK, where do we move on to next?" I asked.

Colleen seemed deep in thought and I felt that she had

not really heard what I had said to her, which was borne out a moment later.

"Cris, you remember what Uncle Fredericko was saying last night about his business, the things he dealt in? What if we were to import some into the UK, to make some money?"

Well, that was a direct approach if anything was. It certainly put me in my place with my 'shall I, shan't I'. A very typical Colleen statement. Perhaps this was why we were attracted to each other. We were very alike in many ways.

I had a funny feeling this conversation was heading in the same direction that I had spent the last twenty-four hours thinking about.

"What sort of things are you thinking of? I imagine you mean the Colombian craftwork." I said slyly, trying to avoid the subject of cocaine and making Colleen actually state her case.

"No, actually it wasn't that, it was cocaine." She said with a sheepish smile.

"Uncle Fredericko could help us at this end. It would be jolly exciting and we could make heaps."

"How do you know that Fredericko would help? What about the risk of getting caught? You have never spent time locked up in prison. It's not an experience I would wish you to try. Who would we sell to back in UK? How would we get it there? I don't think you have really thought about it at all."

I was trying to be as off-putting as possible, but it was extraordinary that we had both had the same idea quite independently of each other.

"Actually I have already spoken to him, before he went to the office this morning. I know there would have to be a lot of planning, but we could look at the possibilities of doing it, and if it seemed too difficult we could always stop and go off on our travels as we had planned."

What a devious little minx she was, though I had followed just the same course.

I could now understand why Fredericko had not seemed surprised when I had come up with the same idea. I decided that for the time being I would not let on to Colleen that I had had the same thoughts, and just see whether she had thought the thing through at all. She was certainly a chip off her uncle's block, if that were possible.

"Right, just for the fun of it let's think how we could do it and market it when we got to UK. What sort of quantity are you thinking of, and how would we pay for it here, presumably to Fredericko, seeing he is already in the business. Have you considered what would happen if we got caught? It would be a long spell in jail which I can tell you, you would not enjoy." I was determined to rub this side of the possible operation in as hard as possible, so that she realised the risks and did not get carried away with the idea of making money.

"I think you feel I am being stupid, which perhaps I am, but I want some excitement in my life. I think trekking round with Julio and his gang got my adrenaline going, and it really gave me a buzz which I want to go on, probably rather like what Rogero and Juanita said they got from sniffing cocaine. How much we would smuggle would depend on how we did it. Uncle did say he could supply it for us, and that it would be quite independent of his organisation and not in a territory that he ever uses for his business. You have money and I have some which could be used for buying, which we could get transferred to here. We would have to see how much we could afford to spend and what quantity that would buy."

"You really are keen on this idea and have thought quite a lot about it; I am surprised. I think the next thing should be that we have a talk to Fredericko and find out what price we would have to pay. How we move it to England depends on the quantity we are dealing with. We will try and get him on his own again this evening. I must say the prospect of making a lot of money does appeal to me but I am not so keen on doing it by selling drugs: they can ruin a lot of lives."

"Yes I know, but if we didn't do it someone else would. I haven't been top of the pile of goody goodies recently and your past is not exactly lily-white! Right, I will race you two lengths of the pool!" She was away in a flash before I was even off my lounger, and into the water in a curving dive with a splash as her bikini top came off, but not stopping she was away up the pool. I was close up behind her at the turn, and half way up the second length was able to catch her leg and pull her to a stop and underwater for a kiss before we both had to surface spluttering for breath.

"Hi children! Would you like a drink?" Pedro was standing on the side of the pool enjoying our fun and games. Colleen quite unashamedly pulled herself out of the water to sit on the side of the pool at his feet, while I retrieved her top for her. Pedro was admiring what he could see. It was just as well he had a long really cold drink in his hand to cool his Latin ardour.

"Yes please, that would be nice, cold and fruity. You're back early today."

"I am going out with a group of friends this evening to a club. Why don't you join us?"

"No thank you, not this evening, we want to talk to your father about our plans for the future."

One thing I had got settled in my mind was that whatever we said to Fredericko, and any plans we made subsequently had to be kept to the minimum number of people. While I liked the Gonzales boys I would not trust them an inch where money was involved.

Chapter 14

After supper we went with Fredericko to his study for a quiet chat. The boys were both out and Mama had departed upstairs to sort out her clothes for a lunch function she was to attend tomorrow, so we knew we would not be disturbed.

Colleen came straight to the point.

"Uncle, we have talked about my little plan and I am very keen to research it to see the possibilities. Cris, I think, is not so enthusiastic, but we need some information from you before we can go any further. Firstly, would you be able to supply us with the cocaine? Next, how much would it cost? As we don't have unlimited money, can you give us an idea what we would sell it for in England?"

"Heh, you want to suck my brain empty of all this information! I thought this was your operation, not mine! Well I suppose I have to help my one and only pretty little niece or else you will get into much more trouble than you will probably get into anyway. To answer your questions. Yes, I can arrange a supply of cocaine for you, it will cost you $250, that's about £150 for a kilo. That is for good stuff of 80% purity. When, or if, you get it to England, that quality could be diluted, and a kilo should sell for at least £6000 on the street to users. You would have to sell to a dealer so would get quite a bit less. There are the costs of getting it to England. Have you thought how you would manage that?"

I had been doing some quick mental arithmetic while he spoke.

"Say we were to buy 100 kilos from you, that would be £15,000 and it might cost us £10,000 for transport, a total of £25,000 which would be worth £600,000 on the street, or say £300,000 to us, less the costs: A profit of £275000."

I could see Colleen's eyes getting wider and wider and her head ticking over like a cash register. This was serious money and certainly put a somewhat different light on the risks I had been worrying about.

"I think perhaps you are being rather optimistic in your calculations. The transport will cost you more than £10,000 I am sure, but then perhaps you have some special plan to get it to wherever you have a market." I felt he was being rather sarcastic, but perhaps he was just trying not to encourage us.

"You understand that the price I can sell to you for is very cheap. It would be the cost of the leaf and processing only. I make nothing from it. I will not lend you any money for this venture as I would really rather you did not do it, and it is once only I will do it for you. Don't come asking me again if you are successful. Probably you will both end up in jail."

We talked generally about cocaine for a while before leaving Fredericko, to wander outside through the garden to decide whether to go further with the venture.

"What do you really think, Cris?"

"Firstly I have to admit to you that I also had this idea, and went to have a chat with your uncle before lunch, but he did not say you had already talked to him about it. He seems to be able to keep a secret." I said with a rather lopsided grin, not knowing whether she had guessed or not.

"You bastard. You made me go all through plucking up courage to tell you this afternoon and you never let on. How could you!"

She had stopped and turned towards me with a hand on my chest and I prepared myself for an onslaught but only received a gentle slap on the cheek followed by a hug. She was so unpredictable.

"Well, now you have made your confession, what do you really think?"

"It would be a big investment for a big risk but with potentially big returns. The adventure would certainly give you the buzz you are after. If you really want to do it I will come along with you on a fifty/fifty basis as partners. I am not entirely happy with the idea though. Can you raise your share of the costs?"

"No, I can't possibly find the sort of money you were estimating, unless I sold my house, or I could go back to my profession and double or treble my prices." She smiled sweetly at me, knowing perfectly well that I would not approve of that option.

"Perhaps we would have to take less weight. That would be a pity though. Do you think I could persuade Uncle to give me a loan repayable when we sell?"

"No, I don't think you should even ask him. He was quite definite on that, and however much you made eyes at him I am sure he would not budge. So it looks as if you are out of the deal, but I might let you come along for the ride just so you could have the adventure you yearn for." I said seriously.

For a moment Colleen's eyes smouldered with disappointment and anger as she turned to me, and then suddenly she realised I was teasing her again as she looked me straight in the eye.

"What is today? Be unkind to Colleen day or something? Cris Barnard, you will push me too far one day and regret it when I stick a knife in your ribs, or tell you to leave. Remember my Latin temperament."

"There's not much chance of me doing that! You are the way to getting the cocaine and that's all I am interested in."

I put my arm round her shoulders and pulled her to me as we strolled on. I had no intention of losing this girl, who had become very attractive to me since I had first met her so many weeks before. Thank goodness it was the doorstep of 9 Meadowsweet Road I had turned up on. Fate had been kind to me that day.

"Well, now I've been told I might get a knife stuck in me, I suppose I have no option but to bank-roll the whole thing. What will be your contribution?"

"It's obvious, I should have thought. As you have said my contact with Uncle, my charm and beauty, and all the many other assets I have! Not to mention the fact that you are stuck with me whether you like it or not."

"OK, now let's be serious. I can get the money transferred electronically; that's no problem. It will take a few days as I would need to sell some investments. I wonder if there would be any queries about moving a large amount of money to Colombia? We would not want the tax people or Customs poking their noses in. Any ideas about moving the stuff from here or wherever we collect it from Fredericko? How are we going to get it into England? Are we going to take it and sell it in England? How do we sell it once we get it there? There are an awful lot of difficulties to the operation. If any one of them goes wrong then we are locked up for a long time."

"I am sure Uncle will help us within this country, but the fewer people who know what we are doing the better. For instance I don't want the boys to know if possible, and no one must have any clue what happens once we leave the country with it. I have thought about how to move it from here to Europe, by sea. Uncle told us that he has a legitimate trade in coffee, rubber and craft items. We find a ship carrying these exports to Europe and include our goods with them disguised in the same packaging. Next we must ask him when he has a consignment going out and where to. Then we have to think how we will move it on."

"That sounds fine if you can get him to agree and he says

the ship's captain is trustworthy. I think it important that wherever we land the stuff is not some big port where the customs will be more vigilant. Why don't you see if he is still in his office? Strike while the iron is hot; I will wait for you out here."

I sat down on a swinging seat by the pool and immediately started having misgivings again. However, I had said I would go along with Colleen so must not now change my mind. Ten minutes later she was back with a big smile on her face, as she plonked herself down beside me, so I knew that the wheels had already started to turn. I was committed.

"That was quite easy! He has a small ship leaving in about four weeks calling first at Oporto, in Portugal, with a cargo principally of coffee packed in bags, before moving on to Cork and Felixstowe. The cargo is mainly from his company but he does share the hold space with two others. He has used the ship and captain before for contraband but not for cocaine. There would be no problem in getting 100 kilos in time for loading, and it would be easy to include it with the rest of the cargo when the ship is loaded. The authorities are not very strict at the ports here in Colombia."

"Right, next we need to meet the captain and agree terms. While we travel to the port to see him we can decide on where to off-load and how we go from there. This is all going too well, I do believe you had it all worked out with Fredericko long before you told me. You are just a scheming little criminal and I think you want me along just for my money. Probably I will be dropped as soon as you get to UK and run off with the goodies. Incidentally, where does this ship leave from to start its voyage?"

"You don't really think I would cheat on you, do you?" She said all seriously, obviously quite concerned at my remarks.

"Yes, I believe you would! But just remember I am army trained and you would have to be watching your back the whole time; you could never relax!"

She turned towards me, frowning with a worried

84

expression. I liked this look as it made her nose turn up at the end, and she looked all innocent and girlishly young.

"Cris, I would rather forget the whole thing than to have you thinking that of me. Surely you trust me? I trust you not to do a runner on me."

I realised I had gone too far with my teasing. It was just that she was too gullible and I could catch her out every time. I put both arms around her and looked hard into her eyes. I hoped I had not hurt her.

"I am sorry. I must not tease you all the time. If this thing is to have a happy conclusion of course we must trust each other implicitly." Before she could say anything I kissed her long and passionately. As we broke apart I think we both realised that our relationship was more than friendship.

"The ship leaves from a place called Barranquilla up near the Venezuela border on the Carribean. It's quite a big port apparently. The captain is called Senor Zacapa and is Cuban. It is only about 1000 tons and quite old, called the "San Jose"."

Overnight I am sure Colleen was thinking about the next step of the plan. I certainly was as I went to sleep and it was my first thought on awakening the next morning.

Chapter 15

Over breakfast I informed everybody that we were going to have a few days exploring the Caribbean coast and would be catching the train to Barranquilla.

"Come along to the study, before you go, for a moment" said Fredericko. "Pedro, Rogero, I will see you at the office very shortly. I need to discuss the state of the market for the next coffee harvest and hear from you the deals you have been able to make so far. I won't be long."

We packed our rucksacks with the minimum we would need for the next few days, said our goodbyes to Mama and knocked on the study door. I felt rather like a naughty schoolboy having been summoned to the headmaster's study. Something I had had quite a lot of experience of during my supposedly formative years.

"Hi, come in. I have guessed you are going to Barranquilla to check the place out. I have written you an introduction to Captain Zacapa. You will have to bargain hard with him. He will not let me down, but his crew are the dregs and could get up to anything, particularly the mate, so be careful."

We arrived in Barranquilla after a long, hot, crowded journey, and were relieved to find a rather seedy guest house near the centre of the city.

We took a taxi the next morning to the docks main office

to enquire about the "San Jose". It was a frustrating search, being passed from official to clerk and back again with total disinterest from everybody. We did eventually establish that there were at least two ships of this name which called regularly at the port, one of which was moored at the far end on Pier 8.

This seemed to be quite a big port and was the outlet for Colombia to the Atlantic and the lucrative markets of the east coast of America and Europe. The docks were a warren of large warehouses on each pier. Completely the right setting for our nefarious business, and just what would be on some gangster film, so we felt we were in the plot and could expect a car chase to come round the corner at any moment. Certainly not the sort of place to be at night on your own.

Pier 8 was where the smaller ships appeared to dock. This "San Jose", registered in Georgetown Guyana, was the last of five ships moored on each side of the pier. They all looked as if they were coastal traders and not capable of crossing the Atlantic, and I felt this rust bucket was the wrong one even before we crossed the shaky gangplank. We were met by a negro in a dirty vest and torn jeans. Colleen asked to see the Captain, to which she got no reply other than an indication to follow him. We were shown to a cabin door below the wheelhouse and left standing; I knocked loudly and then called.

"Captain, we are looking for Captain Zacapa. Are we on the right ship?"

After a minute of silence the door opened to reveal a wisp of a man who had obviously just been awakened by my knocking. He had just pulled on a pair of trousers which still were unzipped and only held up because he was clutching them tightly; above he wore a badly soiled pyjama jacket. He looked as if he had had a heavy night of drinking, half of which had been spilled down his front.

I prayed to myself that this was not Captain Zacapa, in

spite of our frustrating search. If this was him then we had to do a serious rethink of our plans.

"Capitano Zacapa is not here." I gave an almost audible sigh of relief. "I am Capitano Mendes, but I know Capitano Zacapa. His ship is not here I think. You ask at the office, but I think perhaps he will be here in a week."

This was spoken in very slurred broken English, but if correct would give us time to explore the coastline on this side of Colombia.

Once back at the office we were more successful in our enquiries, and established from a pretty young receptionist that indeed the "San Jose", the one registered in Havana, should be coming in to load for Miami in five days. It seemed likely that this would be the right ship, as Fredericko had said that Captain Zacapa was a Cuban.

"While we wait, do we go east or west?"

"It really makes no difference; let's head west towards Venezuela and take pot luck."

We found a bus going in the right direction and spent five wonderful days beachcombing, eating and drinking with the locals in little bars, and sleeping wherever we could. This was really what our trip was meant to be all about, not getting ourselves involved in smuggling.

Apart from lying around in the sun all day we did some serious talking, and came to the conclusion that we would offload the cocaine at Oporto. Cork and Ireland had enough troubles of their own and therefore probably a very good intelligence grapevine which could just complicate things. Felixstowe is a major port for the UK and too close to the drug traffic of places like Amsterdam, not to mention the illegal immigrants' surveillance. Transfer from the "San Jose" would initially be by boat and we would then drive it via Spain and France to Brittany. From there we would fly it into England.

This was all very ambitious. The plan was fine, but we had no idea how to execute it.

The other decision we made, after a lot of argument on Colleen's part, was that she would have to travel on the "San Jose" to keep check on our investment while in transit. She really wanted to be in on the action and not sitting on a small ship tossing its way across the pond. Eventually she conceded that it was important and there had to be one of us on board to check the right bags off, or we could end up importing coffee.

We had made the decision to do the research, so reluctantly once again caught the bus and returned to Barranquilla.

We found the same helpful girl at the office, who told us the San Jose had indeed docked that morning and was on Pier 3.

Sure enough there was an "MV. San Jose", registered in Havana, unloading large crates with the help of the dockside cranes. She was about the size I had been expecting: a rusty but seaworthy-looking vessel. A real busy trader of the sea who probably only stayed in port long enough to load and unload. Masefield's wonderful poem describing the "Dirty British Coaster" sprang to mind; this was the Cuban version. She boasted a far superior gangway to the boarding we had done a few days previously, and we mounted with growing excitement.

We were met at the top by a smartly-dressed officer in clean white shirt and well-creased dark trousers. He was one of the tallest and biggest negroes I had ever seen, standing well over six foot six and the broadness of shoulder to go with it. At a guess he was in his early fifties and had an enormous smile on his face.

"Welcome, Cris and Colleen, I am so glad to meet you. Any friend of Fredericko is a friend of mine!"

"You seem to have been expecting us." I said with some surprise.

"Yes. Fredericko cabled me two days ago to say you were coming, and I phoned Jeannie at the office as soon as we docked to tell me if you came in there asking for me. Come into my cabin and let's have coffee."

For five minutes we exchanged pleasantries and we discovered his connection with Fredericko.

"Now, I understand you wish to take some cargo to Europe when I go there in three weeks; have you decided which port? I will be calling at Oporto, Cork and Felixstowe where I will be taking on cargo for my return journey. If you decide to use my ship I will not need to know what it is that you are sending, but I can only assume that it is something you would rather the authorities did not know about, so there will be no formalities of loading manifest or such like." This was said with a large wink.

"I think you must have been briefed about this, and we appreciate your tact. We would like to offload at Oporto. Just at the moment we have not decided how this will be done. The merchandise will be in coffee bags looking like your cargo but will be identifiable in some way. We would rather that this was all kept secret from your crew. The fewer people that know about it the better. The other bit of cargo we would want carried is Colleen. Is this possible?"

"Oh yes, it will be a pleasure. We do not normally carry passengers but she will be most welcome. As regards my crew, I thoroughly agree with you, I would not trust them with anything. They are good boys for what I employ them but would slit a throat if they thought there was something to be gained from it."

"So all that remains is to agree a price. What is this going to cost us? There will probably be six or seven coffee bags."

This was the bit we had been dreading, as we really had no idea what the going rate should be. I was regretting not asking Fredericko before we left Bogota, but at the time had thought we could not make more use of him than we already had. Captain Zacapa gazed up to the deck above as if to gain heavenly inspiration.

"You realise that if I get caught I will lose my ship and

everything I possess, and spend a very long time in jail. I am taking a big risk to help you and my friend Senor Gonzales. I do not know what you are bringing to my ship; seven coffee bags could be a lot of whatever it is and worth much money to you."

"The seven bags will not all be our goods; there will be a lot of coffee mixed in with it." I added hastily.

"I could work my passage by helping in the saloon and tidying up, etc." Colleen bravely offered. Probably not realising what she was saying.

For one second I thought that she could do much more than that to please the Captain and crew, if it were only known! As quickly as I had thought it I mentally slapped myself on the wrist for even thinking such a thing. The operation was definitely off if that was the only way. It did lead me on to wonder whether she would be safe with a whole ship full of men. Mental note: Get Zacapa to guarantee her safety; half the payment on safe arrival at Oporto.

"OK, I will carry your two sorts of cargo for twenty thousand of your pounds; delivered to Oporto. I have a lot to lose."

My heart sank; this was double what we had reckoned to be the whole cost of transport. I could see our profit melting away like snow on a hot day.

"Oh Captain, you are trying to rob us! You won't even know it is there! I don't think we can afford more than twelve thousand." I had known that we would have to haggle over this and hoped that this figure would not put Zacapa off completely.

We continued the good natured bargaining for another ten minutes. All the time getting nearer to a compromise without losing too much face. At fifteen to eighteen I shrugged my shoulders.

"Captain, I don't think we will ever agree. We are going to be left with nothing. I think we will have to find some other means of moving our stuff."

"OK young man, my final offer is seventeen, and that is only because I do it for my good friend."

"This is silly, you are both behaving like children," blurted out Colleen who had been sitting silently looking from one of us to the other as if watching tennis at Wimbledon. "Why don't you shake hands on sixteen thousand and be done with it?"

Zacapa and I looked at each other and both started laughing at the same time.

"Typical of a woman. OK Cris, I agree, if you do. Though what I am to live on when I retire, I can't think!"

"Yes, we can go along with that. I will just take the extra thousand off Colleen's share! But there are certain conditions I must make: Firstly that you will guarantee Colleen's safety while she is on your ship. By that I mean safety in every way; I am sure you understand me."

Colleen was beginning to look daggers at me, but I held up my hand to her; for once she did not interupt, and I continued:

"Colleen, I know you think you are quite capable of looking after yourself, but we are dealing with exceptional circumstances. Secondly, Captain, we will pay you half the agreed money shortly before you leave Barranquilla when we have loaded, and we will require you to give us a signed receipt to prove your involvement, and the remainder into an account of your choice as I see you enter Oporto harbour. You can check the transaction as soon as you dock before we remove the cargo which by then Colleen will have in her safe keeping."

"Cris, you drive a hard bargain, but I understand your terms and accept them. Now let us have a drink to seal the deal."

Over the drinks, in the plural, we arranged the loading date and details and finally staggered off the ship. We were now committed to going. The adrenaline had already started pumping.

Having recovered from the good Captain's generous measures of alcohol we had another more serious planning meeting now that we were committed to the venture. The timing was all rather tight to keep to the schedule, which was controlled by the date that the "San Jose" would arrive at Oporto. The actual purchase and loading on the ship was no problem as she would not be back here to load for the trip for another three weeks. Fredericko had implied that the goodies could be available for us at little more than a day's notice and they could be driven here in twenty-four hours.

We decided that we had to return to the UK to arrange that end of the operation. Consequently, we booked in to become airline "parcels" again, and were lucky enough to secure two seats for the next evening's flight out of Bogota to London. A quick phone call to Mama to say we would be returning late that evening by train, which we caught by the skin of our teeth.

The next morning we were able to place our order for 100 kilos of cocaine with Fredericko and agree that Colleen would return, with the money available for drawing from the bank for its purchase, two days before the "San Jose" sailed. Fredericko tactfully did not enquire what had been agreed with Zacapa other than to establish that we had a deal. I am pretty sure he would soon discover what had been agreed. Equally, he did not ask (and I would not have disclosed) what our plans were once we arrived in Portugal. What we did not know, and it never occurred to me until many days later, was what Fredericko told Mama, Pedro, and Rogero was the reason for our abrupt departure from Bogota.

So it was we found ourselves back at Heathrow by midday the next day.

We had a lot to pack into the next ten days, but first needed a good night's sleep to get over the jet lag which always seems worse travelling west to east: A coach to Bristol, and a taxi to my house from where we could establish a base.

Chapter 16

The good night's sleep was just what we needed. As we enjoyed a long lie in the next morning we discussed how the operation should continue once the goodies had got to Oporto.

The rough idea was to transfer the cocaine from the ship to either a small boat or direct to a vehicle which we would then drive across Portugal, Spain, into France, and up to Normandy or Brittany. We would leave the vehicle there and transfer to a light aircraft to fly it into England. All very simple really, on paper!

At the moment we had no idea of any detail for this plan. It was all very well having the outline for this crazy scheme, but how could it be done? In reality the actions were more difficult than the words.

We eventually decided that the immediate tasks were to find a dealer to buy the cocaine from us as quickly as we could get rid of it; sell my MG sports and buy a station wagon, or similar car for moving the goods, once we reached England. Also to buy a suitable mobile-home for the long journey up through Europe. I had learnt to fly while in the army, so we just had to find a suitable airstrip and a light plane for hire.

All of this should be quite easy, of course!

The vehicles; no problem to buy.

94

It's easy to drive round Europe with 100 kilos of cocaine.

Border Customs; who cares about them?

Light aeroplane hirers will be queuing up waiting to help us load up.

Once we get to UK every junkie will be waiting to buy from us.

What's the problem, who in their right mind would have such an idiotic idea?

I personally was feeling thoroughly disheartened and ready to call the whole thing off, but as usual Colleen was raring to get going and in no way was going to give up so easily.

She had, from her earlier 'business', got to know a couple of guys in the Bristol area whom she thought would be able to give her some leads regarding the disposal of the cocaine. It was a large quantity and worth a lot of cash, so we were not looking for some tout on a street corner. Because of what it was, and the quantity involved, any approach to potential buyers had to be very delicately carried out.

We decided she should go off and make these contacts. I would make the arrangements for the transfer of the money, for the purchase of the cocaine and half the transport fee, to a bank in Bogota into an account in Colleen's name. It turned out to be remarkably easy, once I had spoken to my broker, to sell thirty thousand pounds-worth of shares in the next two weeks. The money would go straight into my current account, from where the required amount could be transferred to Colombia, and the rest available for paying Zacapa on arrival at Oporto.

I would also sell my car for as good a price as I could get, and see what was available as a replacement and get it taxed and insured. We didn't want to be on the wrong side of the law! We would meet later in the day back at the house. I dropped Colleen off in the centre of the city at midday, before going round the car dealers whom I had selected from the yellow pages as being more up-market and hopefully willing to give me a better price.

On second thoughts I decided to go to the library to look on the Internet to see what sort of price I should expect for a four year old MG, just so that I would not be completely ripped off. This proved to have been a very worthwhile exercise, as the first dealer I stopped at would only offer me about half what it should be worth. The third dealer I tried was near the list price, which I accepted, saying I was unexpectedly going abroad at short notice to work, so needed a quick sale. I arranged to return in two hours to collect the cash and leave the car. In the meantime they had the registration book to check out my genuine ownership.

I filled in the time by visiting other dealers and looking through the paper for the sort of replacement that would be suitable for carrying 100 kilos of cocaine; not the sort of details that most manufacturers advertise as being an asset of any particular model!

Three hours later I had acquired a new set of wheels and still had a good roll of notes in my pocket. The car was licensed for six months and the registration document sent away with a false name. I reckoned that the dark-blue six year old Ford Mondeo Estate would not stand out in anyone's memory, but had plenty of load room and a reasonable amount of zip. I returned to base at my house feeling I had achieved a good day's work: We were really getting somewhere and perhaps my depression of the morning was ill founded.

Colleen rang an hour later that she was just about to catch a train to Bath and would I pick her up at the station. As she got in the car she seemed somewhat despondent.

"How did you get on, love?" I asked, longing to brag about my achievements.

"So so. It's really very difficult as the two guys I saw are both fairly shady customers and I am sure into the underworld. They wanted to know, of course, why I was asking questions about selling drugs. They both said they would make enquiries, and I left it they would phone me tomorrow on my mobile. I didn't like to say how much we might have, and of course I would not be drawn on how we would be getting it. It was all very difficult and scary and I wished you had been there. Somehow it's not the sort of thing that women are any good at negotiating"

"You poor thing. I can't say that I have had a lot of experience in trying to sell drugs. Well, you are quite right, as I've said before, there is no loyalty amongst thieves. The sort of people that deal in drugs would think nothing of bumping off their own grandmother, let alone a stranger. Greed is an awful thing. Having said that, I suppose what we are doing is driven by greed! So we can't talk. The bottom line is that we have to clear at least forty or fifty grand to cover our costs before we start to make anything out of it. I think the way to play it is to not sell the whole lot in one go at the moment, and perhaps even sell to more than one person. We'll then be dealing in smaller quantities which may be more attractive to the buyers. This is assuming we can find more than one buyer, or we can increase the amount if we think it's possible."

"I will talk to these guys tomorrow and see what they have to offer. One thing I am relieved about is that neither of them know where I am living now. We must make quite sure we are never followed back here. Anyway, how have you got on? I see this is a new car, so you must have had a more successful day than I have."

I recounted my achievements and we went on to discuss the next bit of the plan to be organised. This was to find a landing strip in the south of the country and a take-off strip and aircraft in France. The latter would entail checking the possibilities out over there, but first we had to get Colleen's selling end of things squared up.

Her mobile phone rang at eight the next morning before we were even up. I kicked Colleen out of bed to answer it; after all it was my house and her phone. She didn't seem to

97

say very much other than the odd "yes", but was scribbling down notes all the time; finally the conversation from the other end must have stopped.

"OK, thanks Al, we will have a talk about it and get back to you; we have other contacts to hear from first. I owe you one Al......... No definitely not like last time! My past life is behind me now I have started a new career. It's more lucrative. Bye for now."

"I gather that was Al. What had he got to say, other than propositioning you?"

"Yes he did. the cheeky bugger. He just said that he had a buyer for our stuff. He kept saying that he did not usually deal in this sort of thing. He wants to meet the buyer and us as soon as possible. No money was mentioned, but it will depend on the quality, as we thought."

"That was a good ploy saying we had other contacts. I suggest we leave it for a couple of days and go and check out the airstrips first. Of course you have the other bloke who was going to phone."

Before we had finished breakfast her phone rang again. Colleen was much more relaxed today and quite happy to engage in some, often coarse, bantering before being able to set up a meeting for three days' time in London.

First we logged on to the Internet to look for small airstrips, flying clubs, or any place that we could set down a light aircraft. I was looking particularly in South Devon, Cornwall, or Dorset, as they would be the nearest to the part of France we planned to take off from.

Chapter 17

We set out mid-morning with several possibilities in mind. Our search had been reduced when I realised that we would have to leave the car at, or very near to where we landed, as we couldn't afford to delay the transfer from plane to car seeing we would be landing somewhat illegally.

We had picked out three sites; near Blandford in Dorset, Dunkeswell in Devon, and in Cornwall near Bodmin, which is where we headed for to start with. A nice easy drive down the M5 and A30 and we saw the sign directing us to Cardinham shortly before Bodmin. As soon as we drove up I felt that this was too public, although the access to the main roads would be good, but a long way from our possible market in London. Perhaps an airfield was not right for us and definitely this one was a bit too far out.

Next on our list, working east, was Dunkeswell: Once again it was too public with an industrial estate built on the old war time airfield next to the runway. I had however noticed as we drove up from the motorway a sign directing towards a gliding club. This could be a possibility.

We back-tracked, following the signs, and eventually drove up a long access road flanked by gnarled beech trees; onto an open field with twenty or thirty gliders lined up on each side of what I took to be a clubhouse and a low shed with a dozen mobile homes to one side. As we pulled up by the clubhouse a plane took off the grass dragging a glider behind it.

"This looks more our sort of place. Let's check it out; I could do with stretching my legs anyway."

"Yeah, good idea. We can walk on up the side of the field and not be in the way. Oh look there's one coming in from behind to land. It's so quiet." Colleen's spirits seemed to have risen. She had been disappointed when we found how unsuitable the airstrips were for our purpose.

The glider, painted a bright orange, came in over a wood losing height rapidly, flattened out just above the grass and after a short trundle came to a quick stop tilting one wing over.

We walked on for another half mile where we talked to the two men operating the winch near the end of the field where it dropped steeply away, giving the most wonderful view south and west over miles of Devon. We gathered that this was the Devon and Somerset gliding Club. The gliders were got airborne either by an aerial tow by a tug aeroplane up to 2000 feet, or with this winch which pulled them rapidly up several hundred feet.

We walked on to look over the edge of the escarpment. All thoughts of the reason for being there evaporated from my mind as we gazed at the magnificent view. Round to the east we were looking across to the Dorset Downs where they joined the coastal hills of East Devon. To the south and west the eye was taken out to the sea, glinting in the sun, beyond Exeter and the blue haze hiding the starkness of Dartmoor. While to the north-west we looked over Exmoor to the north Devon coast.

"What a wonderful place to have a house. I would never tire of this view."

"Come on Cris. We are not here to admire the scenery. Is this any good for our landing place?"

"I think this is absolutely perfect: We have a clear run

100

in from the sea which we can just see over there. That's it glinting in the sunlight. We can land at this end of the field well away from the clubhouse. I don't think the car would be noticed if we left it near the mobile homes while we are away. We could even probably join the gliding club. Let's go back and talk to someone down there."

The fresh air and sunshine lifted our spirits as we walked arm in arm back to the car. Over a cup of tea in the clubhouse we immediately joined the club as learners using false names and gave an address in London. We gathered it would be all right to leave a car here for any length of time. Everybody was very welcoming, here just to enjoy the gliding, and we got the impression nobody would really notice the car.

As we drove back up the motorway we decided that when we returned next time for a lesson we would disable the car and leave it parked out of the way beyond the mobile homes. We could go by taxi to Tiverton Parkway station for the train to Paddington. I would phone to book a lesson in the next few days before leaving the car. Everyone we spoke to was so helpful and friendly; little did they guess the plans we were making!

This had really turned out to be a very successful trip and it seemed like a good omen for the operation. We had had a good day out with a successful conclusion and our spirits were considerably raised, and we felt even more elated after stopping for a good meal and bottle of wine at a local pub.

On arrival home Colleen set up the meeting with Al in Bristol for the day after, which would leave us plenty of time to travel up to London for the second meeting.

Chapter 18

The arrangement was to meet Al and Jo in the Services car park at Gordano, Bristol, on the M5 motorway. We got there in plenty of time and drove down towards the far end beyond the rest of the cars, parking so that we could see the entrance. We really had no idea whom we would be meeting, although Colleen would recognise Al and thought he drove a BMW, but she did not have a strong suit in cars. Of course they might come in someone else's car.

Twenty minutes went by which seemed like a lifetime. We were both feeling pretty nervous about this meeting as it was completely unknown territory for us. Every car that came into the car park was studied carefully. I regularly asked Colleen, "Is that them?" I knew I was beginning to sound bad tempered, though Colleen appeared remarkably calm but did keep looking at her watch every few minutes!

"That's Al's car, I'm sure. Look they seem to be checking the other cars. Flash the lights and see what happens."

Sure enough we got an answering flash and the car accelerated across the car park towards us. As Colleen had guessed the car was a large dark blue BMW with what looked like personalised number plates. They drew up on our offside and the window slid down.

"Get in the back." the passenger said abruptly.

We looked at each other, I am sure with the same thought going through our minds. Were we going to be abducted? We hesitantly got into the back of the BMW. What could happen in a public car park? I for one had been watching too many gangster movies!

I gave myself a mental kick. We had to take charge of this meeting or else they would try and walk all over us. We were the ones with valuable goods to sell.

Only Christian names were exchanged. Al only knew Colleen as Sarah and I introduced myself as Dave. Al had of course been to Colleen's house but had no idea where we were operating from now, so we felt fairly anonymous, provided we were careful.

Al was a well-built, tidily dressed man in his early forties. A prosperous but tough looking character who appeared very pleasant, but I should think was not one to cross. Jo, on the other hand, was small and thin with a weasely face, dressed in a dark pin-stripe suit. Looking as if he had come straight off the set of a Chicago gangster movie, he would have fitted very well on the docks at Barranquilla. After the introductions we got straight down to business.

"What have you got to get rid of?" asked Jo with a pronounced Birmingham accent.

Colleen and I had agreed that she should do the bargaining initially, but we were only poking a toe in the water today just to see what the market was like.

"We could have 50 kilos of cocaine of 80% purity to sell, if you are able to handle and finance that sort of amount," she said, with a superior looking smile in a rather doubting tone. Like me she had probably taken an instant dislike to the little man.

I hoped this was the right approach to take as Jo looked rather taken aback and cross as the implication of her statement dawned on him. Also I felt that he did not like, or was not used to, doing business with a woman and particularly one as attractive as Colleen.

"That's no problem," he replied gruffly. This could have been referring to either the quantity or the finance.

"We can deliver within the next two months to a place of our choosing. I imagine you will want a sample for testing before delivery; this can be arranged."

"Yes of course, that is normal practice don't you know, and we will test the bulk on delivery. I will pay £1000 a kilo if the quality is as you say."

This was a ridiculously low figure and seemed the right moment for me to join the argument.

"Look buddy, you must be living in a fantasy world up there in Brum. That sort of price is just wasting our time. If you can't do a lot better than that you'd better get on your bike and start pedalling up the motorway. I thought we would be meeting with some class. We will not accept less than treble that insult of a price. I will take £3000 and that's giving it away and you know it."

Jo had gone a bright puce colour at this onslaught, his lips tightening into a sharp line.

Nothing ventured nothing gained, so I continued regardless: "Accept that or we go elsewhere. We have other contacts who will be pleased to take something of this quality from us. You are probably only used to dealing in some diluted rubbish. Perhaps Sarah was right, you haven't the cash to be in the big time."

It would not have surprised me if he had pulled a knife or gun. I watched as many other emotions crossed his face. He was obviously keen to deal but did not like being taunted in front of Al and having his bluff called. He had thought that he could put one over on Colleen and perhaps had thought I was her minder or something. I realised that we had to keep the initiative. Al had remained silent throughout, other than to put a restraining hand on Jo's arm.

"Come on Sarah, we can't waste more time here," and I started to get out.

"OK, wait a minute. I will phone you later today."

It seemed that my bluff might have worked.

"If we have not heard from you by midnight, I will offer the goods elsewhere."

We got out. I leant on the door and looked in at Al.

"Thanks mate. We'll be in touch."

Colleen and I went into the Services for a coffee as much to calm our nerves as to make sure we were not going to be followed.

"Cor, I am jolly glad I don't have to deal in this stuff every day. My heart would not stand it."

"Calm down. You did well, but I am not sure he will accept after our insults. Actually do you think you asked enough? Uncle thought it would make six thousand on the street and we should be able to get somewhere near that for uncut stuff."

"You may be right but I just thought we had to find a buyer quickly. Even at that price it comes to 150 grand which leaves us with a pretty big margin over expenses and we still have the other half to sell. They may pay more in London. If Jo does accept, then we will know for certain that it is a low price and can ask more for the rest. We have got to move this stuff quickly and I am sure it is a mistake to try and be greedy."

"Yes, I expect you are right. It's just that I can't bear the thought of that scumbag making extra money out of the deal when we will have taken all the risks. Come on let's go home and crack open a bottle of wine while we wait to see if shit-face phones."

The phone rang at about ten thirty. We had been sitting, waiting and praying all evening and beginning to give up hope. The level on the second bottle of wine was nearing the bottom.

"OK. I will take it at your price. Phone me on this number when you have a sample." The phone went dead and I quickly jotted down the number I had been given. No name, just one terse statement but I would recognise the voice anywhere.

Our meeting in London was in complete contrast. This time we met Stephen and his side-kick in a crowded pub in Soho. Stephen was a tall fit-looking Jamaican, flamboyantly dressed in a beige well-cut cotton suit with a bright blue shirt and gaudy tie.

We introduced ourselves using the same names as at the previous meeting.

"OK man, what's the score?" He came straight out with.

I thought I would slow the pace down a bit.

"I don't know, I was not aware that England was playing the West Indies at the moment. I don't follow cricket that much."

A pretty feeble joke but it seemed to do the trick as he went into peals of loud laughter, sufficient to turn heads in our direction.

"My "cousin" in Bristol said you might have something to sell that I would be interested in."

"Yes, we could have 50 kilos."

"Phew, man. That's really cool. How good is it?"

"80%. Is that any good to you?"

"It sure is. What do you want for it?"

"Four a kilo."

"Man that's heavy." But after only a moment's hesitation: "If it's as good as you say I will go with that."

"Yes, it will be that good, but we don't have it in the country yet. How do we contact you when we are ready to deal."

"Just let my "cousin" know and then I will phone you. Now we will have a drink," and he turned to Colleen. His side-kick was duly dispatched to the bar.

I was slightly nervous about all his good humour, having read about the 'yardie gangs', shootings and killings, but if one wanted to play with the big boys one had to accept the rough with the smooth. We were just little fish in a big pond with some very big sharks in there too.

The other point that crossed my mind was that we had

no idea who this man was. Could he be an undercover cop? There was no way of telling, so we just had to take a chance on it.

Potentially we had now sold the lot, arranged our shipping, but still had to cross two national borders to get to where we could fly it into the UK. It all seemed to be going so easily, perhaps we had not really started on the difficult part of the planning or execution.

Tomorrow we must leave for the continent to recce that part.

Chapter 19

We set about the next project differently. We simply looked at a map of Brittany and Normandy trying to identify small airstrips. The Michelin maps were good as they marked the aerodromes in different categories according to the type of runway: Hard international – too big and public for us, smaller but still a hard strip – also probably too well used, finally what was called a soft strip which had to be grass – this was the sort we needed. In this category there were four possibles that were worth checking out.

We caught the ferry from Portsmouth to St.Malo on a beautiful hot sunny day and thoroughly enjoyed the smooth crossing, relaxing on the upper deck. We stayed that night at a delightful little Pension in the middle of town. We spent the evening soaking up the atmosphere and smells of France and were temporarily able to forget our reason for being there.

Our first call the next day was east to near Avranches in the south west of Normandy. It was well placed on a point overlooking the sea, well out of town, and had a good selection of light aircraft standing on the apron in front of the reception area. Seeing these planes I began to get cold feet about this flying idea. I had learnt some years before while in the army and had since really only done the bare minimum to keep to the conditions of the pilots licence. It was dawning on me that it would be hard to jump quickly into a strange plane at night to fly across the Channel and land on an unfamiliar grass strip.

"Look I am not too happy about this flying. The idea is good but I will have to have some refresher lessons first. The other thing is we will have to time the trip to coincide with a full or near full moon and a clear night to make the landing easier. Actually, I have never done any night flying." I admitted rather sheepishly.

"Heh, you are not beginning to chicken out I hope." Colleen teased me.

I don't think she had any clue to the problems of night flying. Perhaps I didn't realise what I was taking on.

"Not at all. It will be your pretty neck sitting beside me and I don't want to break it by falling out of the sky! If that happened you really would give me an earful. I know what you can be like!"

"You make me sound like some monster."

"Yes you are! No seriously, I do think it's very important. This place looks alright but we either have to fly out to sea and round the coast past the Channel Islands, or fly right across the length of Normandy. I would like to check out the others first."

We back-tracked west to Lannion, south of Roscoff. This was too near the town which I thought made it unsuitable, but it was on the right side of Brittany and only a short distance across land before we could be out over the sea.

West again to the third possibility. I hoped this would be better as I had already ruled out the fourth, north of Vannes, as being too far south. We were running out of options. This one looked on the map a hopeful; it was west of Landivisiau, well out in the country and not too great a distance over land before heading straight out to sea.

We drove up to near the gates, got out and looked in over the perimeter fence. What I could see looked ideal. A small group of buildings with half a dozen light aircraft parked in front on the grass. A grass strip with a tatty windsock. We got in again and drove slowly back past the gate. The whole place looked completely dead. The notice at the entrance, Colleen told me, read "Bodilis Flying Club, flying lessons and plane hire." This would definitely be our exit point from France.

"This should be ideal for our purposes. I don't think we will go in now, it would be better to leave it until we get here. We will have had time to think through how we will carry out this part."

Back to the Cotswolds again for our last bit of organising.

This was to find the vehicle for the long trip from Portugal to Brittany. We had been discussing this over the last few days and had come to the conclusion that it had to be a mobile home. This would mean that we had a degree of comfort and would not have to leave the cocaine unattended at night. It should be possible with some thought to provide a variety of hiding places from prying eyes, though not from a serious search.

The Bristol area seemed to have a good selection of dealers in motor-homes and having visited three we realised that for our purposes it did not really matter what we got provided it was reliable. We would be abandoning it in France on the way back all being well.

We went back to the second dealer we had visited and settled on an Elddis Eclipe 2.4 diesel that had only done forty thousand on the clock in spite of being nearly ten years old. We were told it had had one careful owner. It was in good condition but we had to pay £12500 for it, serviced with a new MOT, registered and insured, once again in a false name so that the trail would not lead to us when the police started to make enquiries. It was beginning to get difficult to remember all the false names we had been giving and fit the name to the right location! If we were confused, then hopefully everybody else would be more confused.

We were beginning to run out of time for Colleen to get back to Colombia to pick up the goods from Fredericko and get them on board the "San Jose".

There was one last job to do that required both of us before she left. That was to leave the car down at the gliding club ready for our getaway when we flew in from France. I phoned the gliding club to arrange a lesson for Colleen the next day.

We drove the car and the mobile-home, which we had started to call the van, down to Tiverton Parkway station, dropping the van off temporarily while driving on to the gliding club and arranging to leave the car there as we had discussed before when joining the club. Colleen had her lesson in a two-seater pulled up by the winch to about 2000 feet before slipping the tow. She arrived back down half an hour later really thrilled with the experience.

"I know what I am going to do with my share of the lolly: That's buy myself a glider. It's just wonderful up there, so quiet and the views are fantastic."

"I know what you mean. I felt the same after my first flying lesson."

We called a taxi to take us back to the station and collected the van. I hoped that if we were remembered it would be assumed we had caught a train.

Colleen flew off from Heathrow and the actual operation had now started, though I still had a lot to do in the next couple of weeks or so. That evening the house seemed very quiet on my own. Colleen and I had been together through thick and thin for quite some time and I realised I really missed her cheerful company. We made a good pair, continually joking and teasing each other.

I threw myself straight into hard work preparing the van for the trip to Portugal with supplies of food and spare parts such as fan belt, radiator hoses etc. The plan being to make the van look as natural as possible. We were after all just a young couple of holiday-makers!

The major work was to plan how to conceal 100 kilos of cocaine. I did not have much idea what sort of bulk it had and therefore how much space it needed; really I was very naive about the whole business, I assumed it would be in plastic bags of no more than 2 kilos. We thought we had been so meticulous over the planning but had forgotten the small, but important, details. I began to feel pretty depressed about the whole thing without Colleen's support.

I phoned her that evening in Bogota, ostensibly to check that she had arrived all right but as much to boost my morale. It was Fredericko who picked up the phone.

"Hi Fredericko. It's Cris. Our little girl has arrived safely I hope. Is she there for me to have a word with?"

She came on the line straight away so must have been in the room with Fredericko. We chatted casually for a few minutes, and then in passing I mentioned the cocaine.

"What size of bag of sugar should I get to put in the van? I want to put everything in its place."

Colleen clicked straight away what I was asking.

"Hold on just a moment while I think."

I was able to hear very muffled voices as she covered the phone. I could only guess that Fredericko was still in the room with her. She came back quickly.

"A two kilo flat pack would be best. I will need space of about 15 x 30 centimetres for my things."

We continued to chat about nothing in particular for a while longer before saying our goodbyes.

It felt a ridiculous conversation to be having as the chances of anybody listening were so remote, but it was worth taking every precaution.

I was going to be pretty busy for the next few days and would certainly not have time to miss "the old girl".

So I had to find room for 50 bags, to be hidden in a space of about four meters by two. Quite a feat, along with all the normal stuff one would expect to find in a caravan. Having used up all the obvious places such as drawers and cupboards where it could be hidden under, or behind things, I turned to the floor and underneath of the van.

This actually would provide quite a lot of space but would need some surgery to achieve it. My army training now became useful as I had learnt metal work and welding as part of the course for a driver in the RASC. A good day's work cutting and fabricating four metal boxes, hopefully to each take six bags, down at a car breaker who for twenty quid was happy for me to use his welder etc. with no questions asked. I brought them home and the next day cut holes in the van floor and fitted them securely in place, well bolted in as it would be most unfortunate to loose them on the return journey. They became invisible once the carpeting was back in place, but might look unusual if the van was given an underneath inspection. I was really quite pleased with myself as I stood back to admire my handiwork.

Colleen should just about be setting sail from Barranquilla, so it was time for me to head south for our rendezvous.

Chapter 20

Colleen and I had arranged that I would meet her at Oporto but as yet I had no idea how the transfer of the goods would be carried out, and had left it that I would hope to do the transfer by boat if it was possible. The only thing we had fixed was that she would phone me three days before the expected arrival of the "San Jose", and it would be up to me to contact her as soon as the ship arrived. Never having been to Oporto, I might find that this tentative plan was quite impossible, so the sooner I got there the better should it be necessary to think of an alternative. The important thing was to get the cocaine off the "San Jose" as quickly as possible before she sailed on to Cork.

To ring the changes this time I caught the ferry at Plymouth for the crossing to Roscoff and was soon on my way the same evening on the start of the long drive down through France and Spain. The van was very relaxing to drive so I kept going till midnight, with a stop for a light meal at a bar in a small village. As sleep began to catch up on me I pulled into a large lay-by, switched off the engine and got straight into bed. This was travelling made easy to have one's own accommodation with one at all times.

Next morning the procedure was reversed and I was soon on my way. The miles unwound gradually and I was well into

Spain by evening and the following day in the Oporto area parked up in a campsite on the outskirts of the city. It had been a long drive on my own and I was thankful that I would have Colleen for company and to share the driving on the return journey.

The following morning, after a good night's rest catching up on lost sleep, I caught a bus into the centre of town and bought myself a map of the Oporto area which I studied carefully over a leisurely coffee and cognac. There was one problem that immediately became apparent. The main docks were not on the river but north west of the city. I would need to find out from Colleen whether they would come into the river, where the port wine warehouses were, or if they would dock elsewhere.

The question was should we do the transfer from the "San Jose" direct from the ship to the van, or would it be better to use a small boat and then later into the van? I had no way of telling how easy it would be to get into the docks (whichever one it was) with the van. It would also be an unusual occurrence that might be remembered and recorded with the registration number. There were too many "cons" for this to work, so it was back to the boat transfer.

The next call was to the tourist office to ask about boat hire. The pleasant lady behind the desk was most helpful and jotted down for me two companies that seemed to have the sort of boat that was hired for holiday cruising on the River Douro. She volunteered to phone them to ask if they had a boat available for a few days, starting mid week. This was a great help to me as my Portuguese was certainly not up to speaking on the phone. She tracked down a boat on her second call at a village called Pedorido about forty miles drive up river and arranged for me to visit later that day.

I was on the north bank of the river and Pedorido was on the south and it appeared that bridges were few and far between on this bit of the river, so I stopped at a village called

Rio Mao to enquire where the easiest crossing would be. It looked from my map as if I was directly opposite Pedorido.

"Senor, if you just wish to visit Pedorido without your car then there is of course the ferry boat. Down the road to the left and ask at the bar Christabel."

Why had I not thought of that? I hoped that my interpretation had been correct.

All was well, but the boatman, her son, was the other side at present so why did I not sit down and have a drink and madam would summon him back as he was probably just sitting in the bar, the lazy boy.

A young healthy looking man rowed up shortly who was very pleased to join me in a glass of wine. I explained where I wanted to go and he rowed me a short way up the river to the boatyard itself. He seemed very happy to wait while I did my business as I would need to return to Rio Mao. The fact that there might be other people wishing to cross the river did not seem to matter. They would just wait and talk to his mother.

The boatyard was an organised mess of boats of all descriptions and sizes which had been hoisted out of the water onto the dock and were in various states of repair or disrepair. On one side of the dock were two small identical cabin cruisers of about fifteen feet long, well painted and neat looking. I hoped that one of these might be for hire as they looked just what I needed. The office at the top of the yard was a wooden shed, the door wide open. I poked my head in and was just able to see the little man sitting at a desk behind piles of papers, books, and parts of engines.

"We phoned about a boat hire earlier, am I talking to the right person?"

"Si, si, Senor, I will show you." He led me out and over to the dock side, much to my relief, where I had seen the cruisers. I was invited to climb aboard for an inspection. She proved to be just the thing for our purpose. A small decked area at the stern from where one steered, with in front a

116

cabin consisting of a cooker, loo and basin, leading into an area with table and bunk seats on each side, with a very squashed bunk at the bow.

The engine was under the deck at the stern and was diesel. I gathered she had a top speed of no more than five knots so was not exactly a getaway boat if we needed to go anywhere in a hurry.

I paid a deposit and left it that I would confirm in the next few days when I had consulted with my wife. The "lazy boatman" took me back over the river and after a further glass of wine with him I returned to the van to wait for Colleen's phone call.

Chapter 21

I got the phone call from Colleen late in the evening of the next day; on a rather broken up line, but considering she was somewhere out in the Atlantic it did not surprise me.

"How's tricks, luvvy duv! We expect to be with you in three days' time, on Friday, so see you then."

"OK ducky have missed you, but have been busy. Where shall I meet you?"

"Oh yes, I had not thought of that. I will be in the town by the river."

"OK, I might see you as you arrive if I am there in time, but otherwise just keep a look out for me."

"Right, look forward to seeing you on Friday. Bye luv."

Hopefully another of these inane conversations would give nothing away on the off chance that someone might be listening in, but gave each of us the information we needed.

The next morning I returned to the boatyard at Pedorido to confirm my booking for the small holiday cruiser, saying that I would pick it up tomorrow midday. I reckoned that I should allow a full day to cover the 30 odd miles down the river to Oporto, it might turn out to be more depending on the twists and turns of the river. This would give me a good half day for contingencies and refuelling etc. I had arranged to leave the campervan in the hotel car park of the next village of Melres, on the pretext that I had to go to Oporto to see friends and found the parking in the city difficult, so would go on the bus. I passed the afternoon getting together some supplies, enough for the "Holiday" boating trip.

I found a quiet turning off the road not far from Melres to spend the night, hoping I would not be in the way of the farmer should he decide that he needed to get to his field. The less contact I had with people, the less likely that I would be remembered if things went wrong. I had already met a lot of people, what with the ferry lad and his mother, shops, various places I had drunk at, the hotel proprietor, not to mention the boatyard man.

In good time the next morning, I had a roll and coffee at the hotel before locking up the van and walking off in the direction of the bus stop for Oporto, which was the wrong direction to that I wanted to go but gave credence to my story.

Was I being a bit paranoid about this secrecy thing? I decided not, one could not be too careful. The more false trails we could leave the better.

Round the first corner I ducked down a side street and back in the right direction. Once back on the road I thumbed a lift in a pickup truck, with a very talkative farmer whom I couldn't understand, back to Rio Mao, where I met up again with my friend, the boatman who ran the ferry service between the villages.

It was pretty hot by now and I was looking forward to my leisurely cruise down river. The boatyard owner gave me a quick run over of the controls with a short trial run. I didn't let on that I was very familiar with diesel engines and had spent many holidays in the past messing about in boats. Off I set with a full tank of fuel and a full bottle of the local wine beside me. What more could a chap want.

This part of the Douro runs through some spectacular gorges with high cliffs on each side, but without a very strong current. The river, over the ages, must have cut its

119

way through the hills on each side. The hillsides where not too steep were covered in row upon row of grapes destined to become port one day. This is the great port growing area. Many of the vineyards, and world-renowned brands, had been established by the British in previous centuries when port was a commonly drunk wine.

After some ten miles the hills gave way to more low lying country. Here the river makes a great bend through over 90 degrees from running from the north east to north west. I slowed and pulled into the opposite bank on the inside of the curve and was able to see the little road that ran down from the village of Medas to the river. I had previously picked this out on the map as being the best place to do the transfer from boat to van. It was quiet and not overlooked from any houses and the road ran very nearly down to the river's edge.

This was a perfect place to stop on our way back up river; transfer the cocaine from the boat to the campervan and return the boat back to the yard. I studied the end of the road through binoculars and was able to pick out a spot where we could run the bows of the boat onto a small spit of sand which was within twenty yards of where I thought we could drive the van. It appeared to be totally deserted except for one small wooden hut which I assumed was a fisherman's store.

I virtually drifted on with the current and the engine just ticking over, and by early evening, when I reached the point where the Rio Sousa joined the Douro, I moored up for the night. Looking at the map I reckoned I had about another 12 miles to the rendezvous point and a day to do it in.

The next day I made an early start and was soon into more urban surroundings as the river meandered its way into the city. The estuary had an almost fjord-like appearance of natural beauty with the houses rising from the river on the north side in terraces of granite and colourful plaster, while to the south the red-tiled wine warehouses crowded the waterfront.

As far as I could tell from the fuel gauge I had used between half and three quarters of the fuel to get down river; going upstream would use more and I decided there might be insufficient to get the boat back up again to Pedorido

I moored up near the Maria Pia iron railway bridge taking the main line between Oporto and Lisbon across the river gorge at over 200 feet. I just hoped I was not in a No Parking zone. I could see no signs and did not plan to be away any longer than I needed.

Why is it, that wherever one is in the world the first person one stops to ask for directions is always another foreigner or a stranger to the area? Also, if you do find a local they don't speak English! This of course happened to me twice. Fifteen minutes later I was able to buy a fuel can and sufficient diesel to get us safely back to Pedorido, and on returning to the boat didn't even have a parking ticket.

I motored on down until I was at the mouth of the river, turned and came slowly back into the estuary. I needed somewhere from which I would have a clear view of ships coming into the river yet would not draw attention to myself hanging around. I soon found the right spot and anchored near a lot of other boats, on the south side in the shelter of a sand spit, from where I should be able to see all ship movements into the river tomorrow. I had no idea at what time Colleen would appear and just hoped it would not be before daybreak, but if it was I supposed she would phone asking me where the hell I was.

I was on deck by first light the next morning with binoculars and a book to hand. It could be a long day sitting in the sun. It was. No sign of them by lunch time, and I was beginning to get worried, wondering whether I could have missed them. No, that was quite impossible as the ship would come in quite slowly. Perhaps there had been a change of plan and they had gone to the other docks. No, I would

121

have had a phone call from Colleen. I even wondered if they might have sunk in the last few days. No, that was stupid.

I then realised that it had been low tide all morning and probably they would need more water to be able to get over the bar at the river mouth. Relief! The main port for Oporto has direct access to the sea. Our ship, being small, was able to get into the river, which was more convenient for the return load of casks of port, and cork. Two hours later they appeared, creeping slowly in and disappeared up towards the first road bridge. The ship looked even smaller than I had remembered from when I had last seen her at Barranquilla, which seemed an age ago, but was in fact only just under three weeks.

I realised that I was really looking forward to seeing Colleen and continuing our adventure together. I had missed her and her continual chatter and the friendly repartee between us.

Chapter 22

Shortly before six I weighed anchor and motored slowly up river to check out exactly where they had docked. I soon spotted them alongside a wharf by the old warehouses I had noticed before; about half a mile beyond the bridge on the south, with the hatches already lifted but no sign of unloading. Perhaps it was too late in the day for the dockers to start or they had an extended siesta, as long as they didn't work all through the night. Our transfer had to be done under the cover of darkness, as it would look very suspicious for a motor cruiser to stop alongside the ship shortly after it had arrived from South America, even for a few moments in daylight. It would be bad enough in the dark. There are eyes everywhere that would see us unloading our sacks.

I cruised nonchalantly, slowly past at about twenty yards pretending to be a holiday cruiser sightseeing round the harbour. I saw Colleen leaning over the wing of the bridge. She looked fit and more bronzed than usual, so I felt Zarcapa had looked after her as per our agreement. I could see that she had seen me but we did not acknowledge each other in any way. I continued on up the river until I was away from any houses, which seemed to stop quite suddenly on the south side, before finding a place I could moor up for the next few hours.

Shortly after midnight I quietly started up the diesel engine and turned down stream with the engine on tick-over. At these revs it was barely audible even from the steering position, all I could sense was a slight vibration through the soles of my trainers. I was really more worried that the white hull of the boat would be noticeable. I drifted down river until I could see the 'San Jose' silhouetted against the lights of the town behind. The river traffic, such as it was, had stopped earlier so I didn't feel too vulnerable without any lights. I was probably breaking the river laws by not showing lights, but what the hell, it was a minor infringement compared to what we were up to! Come to that I was not sure that the boat even had any.

I passed the 'San Jose' before turning in mid stream and creeping back up, all the time edging in towards the ship. Against the current I had to increase the engine revs which produced a soft 'put put', enough to alert anybody who might be about at this hour.

Our prearranged signal if we were doing the transfer by boat was two short flashes followed by one longer one, returned by three short flashes from Colleen. My heart was in my mouth as I gave the signal. This was to be my first contact with the cocaine; up till now it was just a 'fantasy' and I hadn't broken any laws. Now I, as well as Colleen was in at the deep end, though of course Colleen had been living with the goodies for several weeks and had perhaps got used to the feeling, but knowing her, she would be far too wound up to have even thought along these lines.

Thankfully, I received the three flashes from the ship immediately I had given my part of the signal.

I moved in to the side of the ship as ghostlike as possible with the engine just making a faint burbling of the exhaust, and nudged gently alongside where a rope ladder had been let down. A rope dropped out of the blackness above me. I grabbed it and knocked the engine into neutral before scrambling forward to secure it at the bows. A pair of legs appeared over the side on the rope ladder and Colleen was soon down with me, a quick hug and short whispered greeting. I had expected a much more barbed retort, such as why had I taken so long, she had been standing around waiting!

"All OK. You've checked that you have the right sacks?"

"Yes of course, I'm not stupid you know"

This was said in a much more expected tone and I could imagine the look that went with it, unseen in the darkness. It was actually a rather silly question for me to have asked! She had probably been checking the bags regularly during the voyage. I know I would have hardly dared let them out of my sight.

"Who is up there now? They could do a quick swap while we are out of sight. You should have waited to see them sent down."

"Oh I'm pleased to see you too. For God's sake Cris, stop panicking. If you have organised your end of things as well as I have done mine, then there is nothing to worry about."

The conversation ended abruptly there, as the first of the six bags came over the side and I grabbed it quickly before it disappeared down between the two boats.

There was no word or light from above, the bags just arrived in quick succession. I dropped them at my feet as best as I could.

"Six bags. That's right is it?"

"Yes." Colleen replied rather sulkily.

I quickly moved the bags down the two steps into the little cabin. They could remain there until we had made our get-away from the "San Jose" The important thing was to get clear of the ship and the port area. If we were going to be stopped it would be in the next few minutes.

We moved away immediately. The temptation was to open the throttle fully. However, I realised the stupidity of doing this and returned to the slow chug against the stream that I had used on the approach to the ship.

"Sorry luv, I was a bit jumpy back there. Lovely to see you. Really have missed you."

I put my arm round her shoulders as we stood close together on the little deck at the stern. I had the tiller between my ankles and was able to alter course easily by pushing one way or the other.

"Had a good cruise, have you?"

"Yes, five star hotel. Actually it was pretty grotty. Everything was dirty and I spent ages scrubbing and washing my cabin and the saloon. I hate to think what state the crew's area was like. It was just a very boring trip. I should have taken more books. It was all such a rush once I got back to Bogota."

"Was Capitano Zarcapa nice?"

"Yes. He was OK, but he was running the ship, so he was either on watch or in his cabin. Anyway what about you? What have you been up to? Having a nice time with all the pretty Portugese girls I expect."

So we were friends again and continued chatting away while we made steady progress back up the river, thank goodness without being accosted.

I returned near to the place I had moored up earlier in the evening. By this time I was feeling very tired. It had been a long day with a lot of worry and tension.

Chapter 23

The early sun woke me shining brightly in through the open hatch. Colleen had tumbled into the forward bunk in the bows while I had gone out like a light in the bunk next to the table that I had been using before. The couple of weeks we had been parted had not exactly made us shy of each other, but we needed a short while to get "acquainted".

I lay for a while mulling over our plans and looking across to the pile of six bags on the bunk opposite. Padding out on deck in my shorts and bare feet I found a wonderful blue sky above the river mist which was just starting to disperse. The heavy dew felt really good under my bare feet and I decided to have a dip overboard to freshen up. Slipping off my shorts I dived in and it felt really good after the hot day yesterday.

The river here was still tidal so hopefully not too polluted, it looked clear and clean. The water was surprisingly warm as I swam away from the bank; as I turned I saw Colleen's lithe figure diving in from the deck, her naked tanned body catching the sun, her head coming up half way towards me shaking silver drops of water from her hair. We swam together for a few minutes against the current to stop ourselves being taken down river, then I hauled myself back up over the side onto the little deck at the stern.

"Give me a hand will you" she asked as I came back from the cabin with a towel round my waist.

"You shouldn't get into situations that you can't get out of. I have decided to leave you there and go off with the loot! Of course you might have a bit of explaining to do seeing you are swimming in your birthday suit!"

"You bastard, come on help me out, I'm getting cold, … please Cris."

I relented, grabbed her hand and pulled her up in one swift movement which inevitably brought us close together face to face. I was glad I had had time to slip the towel round my waist! Or was I?

She gave me a quick peck on the cheek and turned away to the cabin to emerge a couple of minutes later dressed in colourful short shorts and loose shirt.

"You wouldn't really have left me in the water, would you?"

She asked this half seriously with a slightly worried look on her face. It was not surprising that she should be a little concerned about her safety at this stage, as the part of the operation that really needed her was now over and I could jilt her of her share so easily. Come to that her Latin temperament could stick a knife in my back at any time. She had had plenty of time during the voyage to ponder and think about all of this, although she did not have any financial stake in the operation. Trust was the name of the game, and my growing feelings for her would never let me desert her. Maybe she was not aware of this. Putting my hands on her shoulders and looking her straight in the eyes, which as usual had the effect of making me feel all gooey, I said "No of course I wouldn't. We are partners together in this. I know we are breaking every law there is, but my motto is honour among thieves. Whatever happens you are my number one concern."

I gave her a quick squeeze of reassurance and a big smile and we let the subject drop. It was not something that had even crossed my mind. She was too important to the job and to me as a person. Hopefully this little incident would 'rebond' us to the teasing happy relationship we had before.

The day passed with the slow sputter of the engine exhaust the only sound to break the tranquillity. There was very little activity on the river. Occasionally we would pass other small boats and once a barge loaded with casks on its way down to the great warehouses. One half of me wished that we did not have our illicit cargo onboard while the other half looked forward to the cash we would collect if all went well and we passed 'Go'.

It was certainly slower going against the current which was deceptively strong. However, by teatime we had reached the great bend in the river and the spit of land where I had planned to do the transfer. I anchored in shallow, still water just short of the spit and slipped over the side with my shoes in hand.

"I've got to go about three miles up the road to Medas, where I hope I can get a lift on to Melres where I left the van, otherwise it's going to be a long hot walk, so I have no idea when I will be back. The anchor seems to be holding all right so you shouldn't have any problems, but you know how to start up if for any reason you have to move. I will meet you here whatever happens."

"OK, have fun. I am going to lie in the sun and be lazy. I will put together some pasta or something for when you get back. Bye."

The three miles up hill seemed like three hundred in the heat of the last of the sun, I was also physically and mentally exhausted with the anxiety of the last few days. Over a cold beer in the bar at Medas I discovered that there was a minibus due shortly that would take me on to Melres. Mother luck looks after the good—I now had time for another beer too!

An hour later, as I was beginning to think it would never arrive, round the corner wheezed a dilapidated minibus. I was not surprised it was running late, it looked as if it would need pushing up some of the hills.

I was glad to get out of the fumes when I eventually arrived safely at Melres, along with a full bus of non-stop chattering women and including a crate of chickens and two dogs. The van was in the hotel car park as I had left it on Wednesday. When I went in to try and pay for the parking space Madam at the hotel insisted that I should come in for a glass of wine; it would have been very rude to have refused! I hoped I wouldn't meet the law as I drove back to the river as I wouldn't have passed a breathalyser test after several beers and glasses of wine.

The journey back was much easier. I left the van at the bottom of the road and walked out to the spit of sand. The boat was there as I had left it; I took my shoes off and paddled out to it. No sign of Colleen at all, I hoped all was well. I climbed over the stern and was relieved to find her asleep in her bunk, quite oblivious to the world. She looked very young, vulnerable and pretty with her hair tumbling over the pillow.

"Come on, sleeping beauty. The man of the house is back and wanting to be fed."

"Oh go away, I was just in the middle of a lovely dream."

More seriously I said, "You really should have been keeping a lookout. Anything could have happened or someone got on board, just like I did."

"Well, I haven't seen anybody since you left and felt really bored and sleepy after last night. You've been drinking anyway. I can smell it on your breath. You've been having fun."

"I would have swapped with you gladly. Walking miles up hill in the heat. Yes I did have a drink or two and you told me to have fun. Now where's that pasta you promised me. Come on woman, to your duties."

I gave her a smack on the bottom and she went dutifully off. Much to my surprise!

It was now nearly dark, but I thought it wise to wait for a couple of hours until it was quite dark before doing our change over from boat to van.

We were both tired so, after a recce to make sure there were no fishermen or lovers in cars about, we went over to fetch the van earlier than we had planned. It was rather rough ground but firm, so with Colleen picking out the route using the torch I drove slowly down to the water's edge without using the lights.

I waded out to the boat, started up and drove in towards the sand spit as slowly as possible, the engine just on tick over and barely enough to stem the current which was pretty weak this side of the spit. I felt the bows ground and the boat stopped; I quickly slipped the engine into neutral, leapt over the side and dug the anchor into the sand to stop us drifting away. Colleen got in and humped the first sack up onto the side.

"You OK with those, they look as if they are quite heavy?"

"I bloody well should be OK with them, I was humping bags of coffee around in the hold in stifling heat checking where our bags were for most of yesterday morning. You thought I had been on a cruise all the time, I suppose."

I had been in such a nervous state last night when we had chucked them down into the cabin that I had not stopped to consider them at all.

I could understand now why she had snapped at me yesterday when I came alongside the ship.

She went on: "What with that and fighting off the first mate who was trying to get in my knickers for most of the voyage, clearing up behind the pigs in the saloon and making endless cups of coffee. It was fun," she said sarcastically, between grunts and deep breaths.

I carried the sacks of coke the twenty or so yards to the van and just dumped them in. We could sort them out into their hiding places later.

131

I was quite glad when the sixth sack was safely in the van. Wading and running through the sand for that distance with 70+lbs on your back was not what I had been used to recently.

"Start up the engine and let's see if we can get this tub afloat again, don't rev up too much."

I put the anchor onboard, put my shoulder to the bow and shoved as I felt the vibration of the engine... Nothing happened.

"Give it a bit more wellie and let's try again.

"Oh God, we will look silly if we have got it stuck, and with a van full of cocaine standing next to it."

A small apologetic voice came from the cockpit

"Sorry, I had put it in forward rather than reverse."

I didn't have the breath left to make any comment. My next shove left me flat on my face in the water as she slid easily away into deeper water, just like a cork coming out of a bottle. As I picked myself up I could hear subdued giggles coming from the boat. I swam out to where she had stopped.

"Here, give me a hand up."

I stretched my right arm up and Colleen grabbed hold of it, with one heave I caught her off balance and she came flying over the side into the water beside me.

"That will teach you to play games with me my girl!" I pulled her to me and we kissed.

"Were you planning to return the boat to its owner or just let it go on down to the sea?" She said as she looked over my shoulder.

The current had caught the boat and it was rapidly disappearing into the darkness while we dallied in the water playing our games. I quickly swam after it and brought it back to anchor in the shallows as we had done last night.

We changed into dry clothes and went to stow the cocaine in our various hiding places in the van, and filled the boxes I had fixed under the floor, which I had constructed while

Colleen was on the high seas. They were just the right size to take six bags each as planned. All should be well, provided we were not searched properly, as the bags of cocaine were scattered around in all sorts of places like under the mattress of the forward bunk or the odd bag in with the groceries or in amongst our clothes. The fifty bags of cocaine did not look like £350,000 but that's what we should collect. I had never seen cocaine before but it looked very normal, like large plastic bags of icing sugar.

It seemed an awful waste to throw away the good Colombian coffee beans which had served so well as a disguise for the cocaine in the sacks. We had over 300 kilos to get rid of and the obvious place was to tip them in the river and let them float away. I could not resist keeping 5 kilos or so to enjoy once we were back home.

I fell quickly asleep in the van as a guard, while Colleen slept on the boat in case it dragged its anchor during what was left of the night.

Chapter 24

Reversing the journey I had made a few days before, I continued on up the river the next morning to return the boat to Pedorido. Meanwhile Colleen had a leisurely day to drive the short distance to Rio Mao which I could reach by ferry from the boatyard. We had no definite schedule to keep to other than to be ready to fly from France with a full moon. We could take our time over the next part of the operation; we had two frontiers to cross before we could get into France and these would be the next worry points: Should we play the innocent English tourists in their campervan, or should we try and creep over on some small back road? In our favour was the fact we would be crossing from one EU country to another and so hopefully not be worthy of close inspection.

As I chugged up river I mused on these alternatives, coming to the conclusion that we should leave Portugal by small roads, but cross from Spain into France at a main crossing, as the French might be more thorough because of the Basque problem in the south west. We could also drive across the north of Spain and make the crossing through Andorra or at any other point.

By the time I reached the boatyard I had made no clear decision other than that I needed to have a serious planning meeting with my partner.

After once again dragging the ferryman out of a bar, I met up with Colleen as we had planned. We moved on in a north easterly direction with still no clear idea of how to tackle the next part of the trip, so after twenty miles or so we stopped off the main road on the banks of the river Tamega, one of the great tributaries of the Douro.

"Let's have a conference with the map and decide how we are going to get out of Portugal. I am in favour of using a small road up in the mountains. Preferably a crossing that doesn't have a Customs Post, if there is such a thing," putting into words my thoughts of that afternoon.

"Is that a good idea, as we will be much more noticeable; but you start looking at the border on the map from the north east corner and I will work towards you from the sea."

Colleen, as always, was systematic and thorough, so we lapsed into a few moments of deep concentration checking the map for frontiers meticulously. Judging by the shading on the map this was a very mountainous area and while there were several rivers flowing across the border the few roads were all marked as having customs posts, except for one.

"I've found it" she said in a rather hesitant voice. "There's a small road marked going from this little village of Soutelinho da Raia into Spain to Videferre. Let me look at the legend on the edge of the map to see what a thin purple line denotes. Oh shit, that's only a footpath. We must look for a thin double purple line."

"I think we have to choose better than that and take a secondary road, and there aren't many of them. Do you think the Customs will be more diligent on a small road through boredom than on a main road."

"No, not if we behave like tourists and I can get them to chat in Spanish and perhaps flirt a bit."

"Well don't lay it on too thick or they will have you for soliciting! These are strong Catholic countries where religion is most important to them and they don't take kindly to being chatted up by an old hooker like you."

This was received with a right jab to my arm that would have gained admiration from even Mike Tyson. I wouldn't like to be near Colleen when she was really angry!

"I'm not old, even if my morals did slip a little, and anyway, I've given up the game to become a drug smuggler. Led on by an ex con."

"OK all even." We said together and burst out laughing.

"We are an immoral pair, agreed! But let's get back to the drawing board and find another route. What about this one going up from Montalegre via a viewing point to Sendim and on to Baltar. That surely would not cause suspicion."

We left it at that, deciding that this would be as good as any other route. We really were working completely in the dark and could only trust to luck. It looked as if we had roughly 200 kilometres to drive to the border, which we would do tomorrow, and try and cross the following day.

The next evening found us stopped near the big lake of Barragem do Alto Rabagao after driving up the main road towards Chaves, but cutting the corner on the very twisty mountain road to Boticas: A spectacular route which required eyes on the road for the driver all the time. Apart from the hairpin corners one never knew when one might meet a local driver on the wrong side of the road, not to mention the odd tourist admiring the view. In fact there were very few of them passing at all, and this began to worry us somewhat as we might be the only people using this road crossing.

We thought it best not to be too early at the crossing so spent a leisurely two hours in Montalegre buying wine and cheese for lunch and doing the tourist thing.

I think also we were rather nervous about committing ourselves to the customs post, and all it might lead to.

Eventually we plucked up courage and started off up the "too good" road for our purposes.

We stopped for lunch at the viewing spot which had a

superb panorama of mountains and valleys in every direction one looked. We could easily have stayed longer.

There was not much traffic but every now and again a lorry or van and the odd car would pass by on their way to either the little village, just before the border, or going on into Spain.

"I've just had an idea," I said. "There's not a lot of traffic, but what if we wait and get just in front of something else, the customs man might hurry us through."

"Well it's worth a try and can't do any harm. We had better get to the other side of the village though, and then we will be certain that the vehicle is going over the border and into Spain."

We stopped at the top of a slope about half a mile out of the village with a clear view down the road so as to see a vehicle coming up in good time.

"The border must be another mile on, I should think, and round the corner of the next hill as I can't see it."

"I think we had better get out and look as if we are enjoying the scenery."

We lounged against the van with binoculars and tried to look like unassuming tourists with all the time in the world to enjoy their holiday.

After ten minutes or so there had been a distinct lack of any movement on the road below us. This enforced delay was doing nothing for our confidence.

"Typical, we have chosen siesta time I suppose. Do you think there is any chance the Customs officer will be having a sleep," commented Colleen, in a rather exasperated and hopeful tone.

"He might of course close the frontier in that case. We will wait another ten minutes and then go, and hope for the best, I think." It had been my idea so I took charge and made the decision.

Still nothing, so we set off slowly on up the road. As

expected the Customs Post came into view shortly afterwards half a mile ahead on the top of the col.

"Well, here we go. Fingers and everything else crossed."

Colleen took one last look round at the road we had just come up.

"Slow down a bit, there's a van coming up behind. It's just come round the last corner from where we got the first sight of the border."

I started to slow as we covered the last few hundred yards. I was really wishing that I was anywhere rather than sitting here in a van full of cocaine. We must be out of our tiny minds, I thought for the hundredth time since we started this idiotic venture.

"I can't make it too obvious."

We drew up outside the small concrete block whitewashed hut with a tall wireless antenna rising above it, with a lean-to shed housing what looked like a generator and a blue four wheel drive pickup truck marked in white lettering "Polizia". In front of us was a red and white striped pole lowered across the road.

The smartly dressed young officer, in a well pressed khaki uniform, came up to the passenger door obviously expecting to be on the driver's side. Our campervan, being British made, was right-hand drive but here we were driving on the right.

Looking across, I could see Colleen starting to put on her act with a great big smile. Her shirt was not fully buttoned, but decent, if he wished he would have a good view down her cleavage improved by the fact she was not wearing a bra. The shorts she had been wearing all day were very short, showing quite a lot of thigh, especially when she was sitting in the van!

"You are English?" The officer asked in a very heavily accented voice. I could see him trying not to look too hard at Colleen. I hoped she had not overdone it.

"Yes, but I do speak Spanish if that is easier."

The thought quickly crossed my mind that he might feel offended by Colleen, that his English was not being appreciated. Also we didn't know whether he was Portuguese or Spanish, not that it probably made a lot of difference in a border area. At this moment the van that we had seen coming up from the village stopped behind us and the driver jumped out and started talking quickly to the officer, interrupting his conversation with Colleen. I felt sure he was probably local and knew him and was asking to be let through onto the road quickly which would be of no help to us.

However the officer was not having any of it. It sounded as if he was told to wait his turn. The officer turned back to Colleen. I was now just a bystander, but the gist of the conversation with Colleen went roughly like this, in Spanish.

"Thank you Madam, I am sorry for the interruption" glancing back at the van driver with a scowl.

"Will you please step out of the van."

Whether it was to get a better look at Colleen's legs, or was standard practice I had no idea.

"You have to come as well and bring the passports," Colleen said, turning to me with a rather worried expression.

We were led into the office and the details of our passports and the van registration noted meticulously. Not so good if they subsequently wanted to trace us, other than the fact the van was registered in a false name, but our passports would be a give-away.

"I see you have a Spanish name and you speak fluently but have a British passport."

"Yes my family came from Barcelona a long time ago."

Colleen was thinking fast on her feet and doing a splendid job of it, but I decided it was all taking rather too long. Probably the officer was doing delay tactics to annoy the other van driver.

"Please I need to look inside your car."

This was beginning to get rather serious. He had had his

complete eyeful of Colleen's body so why not just let us be on our way. Colleen had even stopped her Spanish chatter as she led us out of the office. The officer was greeted by a torrent of words from the van driver as he emerged, and I thought he probably said something like, "Shut up and wait your turn." This was the high point of his day, I expect, to have two vehicles at his crossing at the same time. I was not so sure now that it had been a good idea to arrive in front of this van driver who could be upsetting the officer who was doing a slow inspection of us to spite him. Anyway, it was too late now.

"Keys for the back door, Cris."

She was miles ahead of me in the thinking stakes. I went quickly to get them from the ignition.

Colleen opened the van door and invited the officer to come in. He followed Colleen inside, had a quick look round, opened the loo door, prodded our bedding on the bunks and then seemed satisfied that all was OK. Perhaps he thought we were carrying asylum seekers. I had not had any trouble when I entered the country on my way down.

"You have been on holiday in Portugal?"

"Yes we have been down to Oporto and are now going back to France to catch the ferry home."

At least that was nearly true!

"Thank you, and have a pleasant journey. You may go on now."

He saluted Colleen with a large smile and one last look down her front!

"Thank you, Officer." Colleen replied with an even bigger smile.

I hoped we didn't give the impression of driving off from there in record time, as I tried to pull sedately away, and we both let out great sighs of relief. I felt as if I had been holding my breath for the last ten minutes.

We were caught up after two miles by the van with the bad tempered driver. I let it go past us by pulling in onto the

140

verge, in spite of the fact that it came hooting up to our rear bumper. This would normally have made me be thoroughly bloody-minded, but on this occasion sense prevailed. We could not afford to get into an argument.

Chapter 25

To carry out the next part of the operation we had to get ourselves from north-west Spain all the way up to Brittany, and of course we had the border crossing to contend with as well. Just because the last one had gone off without a hitch, or rather with only butterflies in the stomach, the French crossing could be another kettle of fish. I realised that we should not feel complacent about it. This was a much more important border crossing, still within the EU, but a major trade route between Spain and the northern countries.

From where we were, just north of the border, to the coast near San Sebastian in a direct line looked pretty impossible because of the very mountainous terrain. There were roads we could use, lovely scenery no doubt but we were not really here to admire the views. I just felt that we needed to get on and get it over with, there was no point in putting it off and we had to do it sometime.

So we made the decision to head north east up towards the coast near Oviedo and hit the main road to take us on to the border near San Sebastian on the Atlantic coast. As we were in no rush we didn't need to drive a great mileage each day, so could to a certain extent try and enjoy the trip, but very much on the top of our minds was the worry of the border. Once again, we as yet had no definite plan how to tackle it.

"Do you think they have sniffer dogs at the border to search out drugs?" asked Colleen tentatively, "because if they do we are really buggered."

"This is a snag that had occurred to me, but I feel it is very unlikely. There was an enormous amount of traffic at that crossing when I came down the other day, both commercial and holiday. I didn't see any sign of sniffer dogs; the traffic was moving through pretty steadily, though I suppose they might check odd vehicles at random"

"It would be just our luck to be picked out. It's all gone so smoothly since we left Colombia that I feel our luck must run out eventually."

"Don't be so pessimistic. After all, we knew the risks when we decided to contact your uncle with this harebrained scheme. Luck is with the ignorant, perhaps, though I do think getting caught and spending a long spell in a French or Spanish prison is becoming less and less to my liking. I must say, now we are in the thick of it I do wonder why we ever set out on such a crazy scheme. It also worries me a bit that we are adding to drug usage just for the fun of the adventure."

"Me too, but I hope you are not going to blame me for dragging you along on this trip. I didn't really think about the risks of this part. I always thought the Colombian bit would be the worst, not that it wasn't unpleasant at times and a worry, and I never felt I could completely trust my Colombian family, but once we were at Oporto and away from the ship I was quite relieved."

"Eh, I was warning you about your family when we were there, remember? No, of course I don't blame you. It's all good fun and excitement most of the time. We could give up now and find a market in Madrid I am sure, but we have no contacts."

"No, not bloody likely. We've come this far and I am not

143

going to chicken out now and lose the chance of making a real bundle."

"It's funny the way greed and crime seem to run in families. In your case it must be generic!"

"You know, Cris, sometimes you can be a real bastard. You seem to be forgetting that you have spent a spell in prison. So, talk about the pot calling the kettle black. Also we were not all born with a silver spoon in our mouths."

"Ooh, I have hit a raw spot. You know I was only joking."

"I hope so. Anyway we go ahead with this. I don't like not finishing a thing I have started."

Colleen was a very determined young lady, and even the thought of prison was not going to put her off!

"The other option is not to cross on the main road by the coast but to look for another country crossing. Or we could drive across to the Mediterranean side and cross there, but I think it would be just as busy."

"No I think we stick to the original plan such as it is and go for the route this side."

So we did just that, and after three days of driving we found a campsite near San Sebastian, ready to take the plunge the next day.

Neither of us slept well that night. I could hear Colleen tossing and turning in her bunk, and all sorts of thoughts seemed to be racing through my mind all night. Consequently we were both ready to rise early for coffee. I really had no appetite and was feeling very jaded from the disturbed night.

"I think we would do best to hit the border late morning or early afternoon when the traffic may be at its heaviest. Unless they are on the lookout for us there is no way that we will stand out from any other British campervan. There is no reason they should be looking for us as we have been completely law abiding since landing, in all respects except one of course!"

I said this trying to boost our confidence.

Chapter 26

It was about midday when we joined the queue of traffic at the border. The lorries, of which there were masses, were diverted into a different stream. As we neared the front of the queue I gave Colleen's hand a squeeze,

"Good luck sweetie, here we go. See you in France."

We exchanged nervous smiles.

"I can't see any dogs. The notice says have your passports ready. I've got yours I think already."

The car in front of us moved on.

I drew up at the customs post, trying to look as nonchalant as possible, whatever that looks like, but probably looking as I felt: Guilty.

The post's window was open and a large ringed hand came out, without any word spoken. My eyes ran from the hand, up an arm rolling in fat, to an enormously overweight lady with a cross, piggy face, complete with the makings of a moustache, staring at us ferociously; badly dyed blond hair growing out at the roots. Eventually, as Colleen was also temporarily immobile, and once again the window was on her side, the mouth opened in the gross face.

"Passports," and the hand waved about impatiently. They were briefly glanced at, the hand came back out with them and we were waved on.

"Is that it? Can we go now?" Colleen asked with surprise.

"Oui, allez."

I didn't quite slam the van into gear, but let the clutch out too quickly and stalled the engine. I could see out of the corner of my eye the look of bored exasperation on the face, and assumed the muttered words were something like, "Les Anglaise …" and then we were away. In France.

We both let out a great sigh, as if we had been holding our breath for the last five minutes. We probably had!

"Oh God, I nearly pissed myself when she looked at me. I suppose she was a she! What an anti-climax after all our worries, and then you went and stalled the engine. We've made it." Colleen was bouncing up and down in her seat, the relief flowing out of her in dollops!

"I can't believe it was so easy. What a relief we are not going to be guillotined. Well, not today."

I felt quite limp with the release of all the nervous tension I had built up over the last twenty-four hours. I felt quite the opposite to how Colleen appeared. I would just like to have lain down in a darkened room.

"I need a strong coffee and a very large brandy. I am going to stop in Bayonne to recover, and we need to stock up on supplies again."

Having recharged our batteries several times, we both felt distinctly sleepy after the disturbed night before and all the tension. We drove on up the coast to a rather crowded campsite amongst the sand dunes and fir trees, which are so common in this part of France.

It was early evening by the time we surfaced, having crashed out immediately on arrival in the campsite.

The next morning dawned grey and windy with a strong possibility of rain to come before long. The campsite was certainly not up to the standard we had got used to in Spain and Portugal. It seemed to be mostly young people, crowded in with small tents who had arrived on motorbikes or small

146

old cars. They were in for an unpleasant time if the weather turned out as I expected. We were on the Bay of Biscay coast here and the Atlantic fronts could come sweeping in rapidly.

There was nothing to delay us here and we still had the whole of the French western coast to cover, with nicer places to stop. Consequently we motored on, keeping off the AutoRoute which runs from the border via Bordeaux to Nantes. We stopped overnight south of Nantes and decided that we had earned a couple of days' relaxation before starting the next phase of the adventure. Colleen picked out on the map a village called Le Pouldu, west of Lorient, it looked small with nearby what appeared to be a rocky coastline with sandy coves. It would be ideal, and the weather was back again to cloudless skies.

We were lucky when we stopped at a farm near the sea to ask about campsites. Colleen was greeted effusively by the farmer when he realised we were British and spoke good French, or rather one of us did! We were instructed to park up in the next field and then come in and have a glass of cider with him.

Monsieur and Madam Forgene were small, round, red-faced people in their late 60's and so welcoming, as if we were the first people they had seen in months. I could see they immediately took to Colleen, as everybody did. I felt somewhat out of it as the three of them chattered away, though I was included from time to time with a translation. I smiled to myself as I wondered what story Colleen was making up trying to explain to them who we were, what she did, were we married (she wore no ring), and just hoped she would remember the facts correctly later and would not be caught out. Gosh, they would have been horrified if they knew what we were really up to.

The Forgenes lived in a small whitewashed farmhouse attached on both sides to the farm buildings and looking out onto a cobbled yard with barns or suchlike opposite. All

147

dating back several centuries, I should think. It was very picturesque, with colourful geraniums growing from troughs and hanging baskets. I could imagine that it would be well protected from the gales off the nearby sea.

The cider could have been used as paint stripper as it was so dry! I guessed made by Monsieur Forgene himself, but the little sweet home-made cakes that went with it were delicious.

Chapter 27

We left the farm after our leisurely two days by the sea at Le Pouldu. It had been a good break that we really needed. The Forgenes had been so hospitable and we felt they had really enjoyed our stay. They were in a way rather lonely, as their family had all moved away to more modern areas with better jobs and more money. Peasant farming was not for the new generation.

Once again we headed north, following the Route National but keeping off the Autoroutes. We were in no great hurry and it was only about 100 miles to our next stop at Maison de la Riviere, from where the next lot of action would be based. I was pretty certain there would be a campsite there. Even the smallest town seemed to have a campsite and/or swimming pool.

The miles slipped by as we headed up towards Quimper and then on through the D'Armorique Hills before turning right up the D18 for the last 12 miles to the destination we had selected.

Tomorrow I should be able to arrange my refresher flying lessons at the little airstrip near Landivisiau.

We woke in good time to rain drumming on the campervan roof. This was a day for doing a recce and making contact with the flying club, so the weather was not important but we had got rather used to the sun and hot days while we were in Portugal and Spain. In fact by the time we got to Landivisiau the rain had stopped and blue sky was beginning to show in the West.

After a few wrong turnings we once again found ourselves outside the airstrip, some 5 miles to the west of Landivisiau; not exactly the most impressive place. I had rather forgotten since we were last here how derelict it all looked; a couple of small sheds or hangars and a concrete construction control tower with a portacabin type building beside it. The car park was rather muddy-looking gravel with a fair percentage of it being large puddles. In fact thoroughly scruffy and run down, but then perhaps this was just what we wanted.

As we drove up towards the control tower we read a notice on the portacabin: "Brittany Flying Club" with a telephone number beneath it; also two cars, a battered old Peugeot and a sleek red Ferrari, and a motor scooter, pulled up in front of them. What a contrast! We could now clearly see half a dozen aircraft parked in front of the control tower. Most of them with tarpaulins pulled over their engines and windscreens. The grass airstrip and buildings looked like left-overs from the war; probably it was a fighter station for our boys before they were pushed out by the Germans at the outbreak of war. What stories it must have to tell and now we were adding another chapter to its history.

I pushed open the portacabin door to find a young girl in her early twenties, sitting behind a desk, with a fashion magazine spread out in front of her half covering a radio set and microphone. This was obviously the flight control room! The concrete control tower was presumably obsolete. The girl had a very limited view of the airfield, but I should think it was pretty rare for anything exciting to happen except for the odd sheep.

It suited our purposes perfectly, as we had hoped from our research.

"My husband wishes to have some refresher flying lessons over the next few days. Is that possible?"

Thank goodness for Colleen and her fluent French.

"I don't see why not, but you will have to see Michel LeGrande, he's the owner and chief instructor, at present he is up with a pupil but should be back within the hour".

"That's OK, we will hang around. I hope that Monsieur LeGrande speaks some English? How many instructors are there here?"

"Oh yes, he has very good English, actually he is the only instructor." She admitted rather sheepishly.

We left her to her magazine and went out for a wander round while we waited for Monsieur LeGrande. Every extra bit of information we could glean might come in useful over the next few days, so we poked our noses in wherever we could. The control tower, as I had guessed, had not been used for years and the hangars looked as if they were only used for storing and servicing the planes sitting on the apron in front of the flying club. It all looked very run down.

We could see a small plane doing lazy circuits in the sky a short distance to the north, and after 40 minutes it turned into the end of the strip before touching gently down and motoring slowly across the grass towards us, parking up in front of the portacabin.

The side door opened, followed by a pair of trainers, long well-shaped legs encased in skin-tight purple jeans, (just my luck that this could not possibly be Monsieur LeGrande.). A slim waist encircled by a broad black leather belt, and next a bright pink shirt, the whole lot topped off by a cloud of blonde hair held back with a matching pink scarf. The whole package as it got down off the wing stood nearly six foot tall.

I got a kick on the ankle from Colleen, "You are drooling, stop staring" she said. I can't think why, I was not Colleen's property and could appreciate a fine filly if I wished!

"Hey. You are not jealous are you?"

In complete contrast, the man who followed her was only five foot six, dressed in crumpled slacks and T-shirt with a jolly round face that looked as if it needed shaving at least twice a day. This, without any doubt, had to be Monsieur LeGrande. I was also pretty certain which car out the front was his.

They stopped to talk and shake hands with us.

"I am Michel LeGrande and this is Mademoiselle Suchard who has just started to fly. I will be with you in a moment."

"Enchanté, Mademoiselle. That was a very smooth landing." I did not quite feel I should bow and kiss her hand, and possibly my greeting was too familiar for someone I had only just met.

I glanced sideways out of the corner of my eye at Colleen. As I had expected, her eyebrows and eyes were trying to go over the "top of her head" in exasperation as she mouthed at me "You creep," or that was my interpretation, but I had to get back at her for the kick on the ankle.

"Oh, thank you. Actually it was Michel who landed us."

They disappeared into the "club house" and shortly we heard the deep engine snarl of the sportscar being accelerated away.

"The car's the bit I would really like to have. Just a tad better than my old MG," I said, trying to make peace with Colleen.

A moment later the door opened and Monsieur LeGrande walked across to join us and greeted us with the usual formal shaking of hands.

"Bon jour, how may I help you? You are English, no? Bernadette tells me you wish to refresh your flying and I would like to practise my English."

His English sounded adequate for me to be able to converse safely with him in the air. I took an immediate liking to this little man. What is it that is so attractive about the French speaking English? Perhaps it is memories of that lovely TV series "Hallo, hallo"! They don't make comedies like that any more.

"Yes please, and yes we are English. We have recently bought a small house at Botmeur, the other side of Commana in the foothills of the D'Armorique. As you can see I learnt to fly some years ago on a Cessna 150."

I handed him my logbook, which he opened and looked at casually while I spoke.

"We will wish to pop over to England fairly regularly, and sometimes bring friends back to stay with us, so will need a plane to carry four, plus their baggage. So what I am after is familiarisation with something that will serve this purpose and which I will be able to hire from time to time. Are you able to help?"

I had got my Private Pilots Licence several years ago when I was stationed up at Catterick in Yorkshire, before I had my "holiday" at Her Majesty's expense. I was an instructor with the recruits' training team there, which I found pretty boring and had decided to make use of the nearby flying club to have lessons. Once I had started I was hooked and after the required flying time and written exams obtained my PPL. This was not sufficient to keep me out of trouble with the subsequent problems. Since obtaining the licence I had only done sufficient hours to keep the licence up to date each year, and needless to say there had been one rather longer gap.

"Please call me Michel," said with a broad grin and another handshake.

"I'm Cris and this is my wife Colleen."

"Come and have a look at a Piper Warrior. The one I have just brought back with Mademoiselle Suchard. I think this would suit you very well. It has a range of over 600 miles and carries four people, so you would easily get over to England. We have two of them here so I could hire one to you without affecting my lessons."

The Piper Warrior looked a sturdy little plane, tricycle

undercarriage with the wings below the fuselage. Looking inside it had two pairs of seats with a small baggage area behind. The controls looked very similar to those I had been used to. I thought it should serve our purpose adequately.

"What size engine does it have?"

"The engine is 160 hp. She will cruise comfortably at 100 mph and climb at 600 feet per minute"

"That is with four people and their luggage?"

"Yes, she will carry a total load of about 900 lbs., so depending on the size of the passengers there is room for lots of luggage. Madam likes to travel with many cases?" as he turned towards Colleen, with a smile.

Little did he know how close to the mark he was!

I did some quick mental arithmetic while he spoke. Colleen and I together probably weighed something like 310 lbs, and our 100 kgs of cocaine would be roughly 220 lbs. so we would be well within the limit. What a pity we had not brought more of the goodies!

It was a relief that our research had been correct. The airfield was quiet, the plane was just right, and I could have my refresher lessons with no questions asked. It should all be "a piece of cake," as the flyboys used to say.

"OK. That should be fine. Now what will the cost of the lessons be?"

"I will have to charge you 165 euros per hour for the lessons, and we will talk about the hire when you are ready but it will be about 145 euros per hour of flying time and depending on how long you would wish to be away."

"That's a bit more than I had expected, but OK I'll go with that."

I didn't want to seem too keen. A little resistance on my part should help to stop any suspicion if he had any, which he seemed a too relaxed and laid back sort of person to have.

"Can I have a lesson tomorrow afternoon? I might just as well get going as soon as possible."

"Let's go in the office and see what's happening. Right, what about three o'clock?"

"Yes that gives us plenty of time for a leisurely lunch and to get here."

"I am sure I don't have to remind you not to have too many glasses of wine!"

"Oh, don't worry Michel. I will ration him to one orange juice!" Colleen joined in the charade.

I got the feeling that Michel was not over busy. The look of the place and the one-man band all pointed to a business struggling to survive. Our little escapade might give him some free publicity and bring in new pupils. I knew that our devious ways would bring some good to someone! Or of course it could have the opposite effect and push him over the edge into insolvency. I hoped his insurance was kept up to date, as I had no idea at the moment what we would do with the plane assuming we made it to the UK.

Chapter 28

After leaving the airstrip we drove north towards the coast to the west of Roscoff, by as direct a route as was possible in the narrow lanes which reminded me so much of Devon. This was the course we would follow when we started our trip to England. I just needed to make quite sure that there were no obstacles such as power lines, hills, or tall buildings that could prove to be an 'embarrassment' so soon after our take off, which might be in a rush, though I sincerely hoped we could creep out unseen.

There didn't appear to be anything to worry about so we drove on to the little village of Dossen with its lovely sandy beach at the mouth of the river. We walked round the point, scrambling over the rocks as the tide was out, to the next sandy cove; a perfect nearly-deserted spot to have our picnic. We had bought paté, cheese, and baguette of delicious fresh bread on the way this morning at the market in Landivisiau; also included was a nice bottle of local red which I was allowed today and planned to make the most of; though as Colleen was partial to a drop of vino as well, how much I would get was debateable. The day had turned out hot again after the rain and we both stretched out on the sand feeling replete and relaxed. I certainly dropped off to sleep for a short while and woke feeling too hot and sweaty.

"What about a swim?" I enquired of Colleen.

"We don't have our costumes, and we are not completely alone."

"I don't think that matters a lot here. I believe you are feeling modest. Surely being seen in the buff by strangers does not worry you of all people, and anyway I can't see that young couple worrying. I'm going to, anyway."

Colleen had never shown any modesty about that sort of thing between the two of us, in fact rather the opposite if anything as she quite often walked round the house with only the minimum of clothes on, and could not have thought twice about it in her past profession.

"Well it's a bit different when it's not one on one which I am used to."

"Ha! That's a good one. Was it an intentional joke?"

"What do you mean?"

"One on one. Your past profession."

"Oh I see, you have a warped sense of humour sometimes, streaker Streeter. OK, lets go for it then, it may wash away some of your randy thoughts."

I realised that she was not amused at my references once again to her past and was now trying to put it behind her. I must try and not mention it again. On reflection I decided that I was probably jealous of the men in her past life.

The sea felt really cold after lying in the sun, so it was only a quick dip, gasp and splash around before running back up the beach, the momentary crossness of a minute ago completely forgotten. I felt a different person and completely refreshed.

"Here have my shirt to dry on, it will have dried again by the time we get back to the van."

We lay again in the hot sun to warm up. There is nothing like the feel of the sun and breeze on one's bare skin and the tension of the last few weeks seemed to drain out of us. The other couple had followed our example and were now playing with a Frisbee without a care in the world. After all this was France. The French are so much more relaxed about this sort of thing than we rather stuffy British.

We soon got onto the main road from Roscoff to Brest and on to our campsite at Maison de la Riviere.

The next day we arrived at the airstrip in good time for my lesson. Michel spent a couple of minutes giving me a run down on the layout of the controls etc, and then somewhat nervously I started up and we were off. It all came back to me as if I hadn't been away at all, as I lifted us up off the strip. I immediately remembered the wonderful feeling of complete freedom that I had always experienced when flying a light aircraft, and that Colleen had enjoyed having her gliding lesson. It was as if one was as light as air and capable of doing anything. I can understand how the early pioneers of flying were so exhilarated by dodging and swooping round the clouds. I sometimes had a dream with this sensation, which on wakening I always felt I had a smile on my face. Package holiday flying is totally different as one is just a parcel being delivered from A to B, and consequently with no control.

We did the usual turns, different manoevres and a bit of flying by compass etc. All fairly basic stuff, but no doubt Michel needed to weigh up my abilities. The hour seemed to literally fly by. My landing was not spectacular! Several rather heavy bounces, and it was not exactly a three-point touch down. However it did prove that this was a sturdy aircraft, which we might be putting to the test in a few days.

"How did it go, luvvy? I thought you were going to collapse the undercarriage when you landed!" She said rather caustically, with a very typically "married" voice.

"A little more practice is required in that department, I think" was Michel's tactfully put rejoinder, especially with a very Gallic shrug of the shoulders.

We chatted for a while about the locality and things in general, before arranging another lesson for the following day.

We had to get the confidence of this man, so that he

158

would feel quite happy about hiring to us. Not that the latest plan had any idea of hiring a plane. We were going to steal the plane for our entry into England. We were already breaking the law, so why not go the whole hog. I reckoned that such a minor offence as theft was nothing compared to smuggling cocaine.

However, it all depended on somehow getting the plane's ignition keys. We could break into the flying school's office but it might be alarmed and I had no idea where the keys were kept. Michel might even take them home with him. If it was me I certainly would, there are too many rogues around.

A plan began to form in my mind overnight, which I put to Colleen at breakfast. We got going on a "brainstorm" session and soon the plan began to develop.

"How about getting an impression of the plane's cabin door and ignition keys so that we can then get our own set cut."

"That's OK, but how will you get a chance to get the impression?"

"We need some form of distraction."

"Could we somehow make use of the gorgeous Mademoiselle Suchard in her skin tight trousers? You men are all the same and completely lose it if you see a curvy wiggly bum. You certainly proved that point yesterday."

"I can't think where you have got that opinion from! But how would we get Michel to chase after her and leave me with the keys for a minute. He's hardly likely to just chuck them to me for no reason. Anyway we don't know when she is having another lesson."

"That's easy. While you are up flying I will chat to Bernadette and when she turns to answer the phone I will casually look at the appointments diary, and see when she has another lesson."

"OK, so far so good. Supposing I fix a lesson to follow

hers, what then. Michel is not going to just stand there with the keys held out."

"Right, here's another idea: Just after you have gone out to the plane and are about to start, with the keys in the ignition, I phone Bernadette in the office and pretend to be Michel's wife needing to talk to him really urgently. He jumps out and comes back to the office only to find that I will have rung off."

"Possible, but there are too many things left to chance, such as you would have to time it exactly to catch us having got in but not yet taken off. Or Bernadette may say he's giving a lesson and can't come to the phone, but will phone back. Come to that do we know Michel is married? It will look very suspicious when he asks his wife why she phoned and she says she didn't. No we have to think of something better than that. There are too many unknown factors. Anyone of which could trip us up. Whatever we do has to be really watertight and apparently completely unconnected to us."

"Yes he is married and has two children, Bernadette told me, but I agree it might be difficult. So what about the glamour puss idea."

We were unable to come up with any more bright ideas but like me I am sure Colleen was mulling it over in her mind.

The lesson that day went off better, or at least the landing was a lot less spine shattering. It was just as well as we had an important need for the plane not to be out of service due to my inept landings.

Once we were back in the van, having made a booking for the next day, Colleen turned to me.

"I think I've cracked it, there is still quite a lot of luck but it might work and even if it doesn't nothing will be lost. We book a lesson for you following 'what not's'. While she is having it, oh god, you men with your one-track minds, there's not room in that plane to try for the Mile High Club!" This was in response to my eyebrows raised expression. "Be

160

serious for once Cris. While she is having her flying lesson we puncture or rather let the air out of one of the Ferrari's tyres,"

"Yes, I get it. Beautiful girl in her posh clothes waggles her eyelashes at Michel who goes to change the wheel for her. OK, but I still don't have the keys. She might also just get on her mobile and phone the AA or whatever the equivalent is over here."

"Don't be such a pessimist. If it does not work then we will have to think of something else, nothing will be lost. If she does get him to help then just ask for the keys and say you will go out to the plane."

We left it at that but decided that Colleen would look at Bernadette's diary while I was up tomorrow.

Chapter 29

The lesson went off without dramas. I was improving, especially as we practised circuits and bumps. To the layman this is landings and takeoffs. I was beginning to feel much more confident about doing the trip without killing us both.

Before I could speak, Colleen broke in quickly "You have remembered we are busy for the next two days, but you could come again later on Thursday afternoon. Four o'clock would be quite a good time. We have that appointment with the notary at two which won't take long, and we can come straight on. Does that fit in with you Michel?" She asked with a sweet sexy smile and her head coquettishly tilted to one side. Who could refuse her? I never could.

I realised that she had obviously got a glance at the diary, as planned. Michel led us into the office and looked at the diary.

The timing was working out really well. The moon would be full in about four days' time so, weather permitting, it would give us the best possible light for the take off and landing. Although I wasn't sure when it would rise or set, it had been well up when I woke in the middle of last night. I didn't know for which it would be the most useful; I suppose the landing at the gliding field, as we had to find the place, let alone land on it.

"Yes that's OK, I have Mademoiselle Suchard at three, so you can go straight after her."

So far so good.

Two days later I cut a small branch out of the hedge behind our van and whittled it down to a point. I just hoped that the Ferrari would have normal valves on its wheels; if it did, then my little stick would be used to push down onto the pin of the valve to release the air.

The next job was to find somewhere to turn our key imprints, if we were able to get them, into usable keys. This would be better if it was done at a distance from the airstrip, so that the theft of a plane would not be associated with keys being cut in this fashion.

"It's a bit of a drive, but let's head for St.Brieuc. Do we go to an ironmonger or a locksmith?"

The ironmonger we found was unable to assist, but was helpful in looking in the telephone directory for locksmiths. Colleen jotted down the numbers and set about working down the list of five numbers. The third she tried told her to bring an imprint in and he would see what could be done. This one was in Rennes, over 50 miles further on so was well off our patch.

We stopped in Landivisiau on the way to the airstrip for Colleen to find a toyshop that sold children's plasticine. She returned shortly with success written all over her face.

"That wasn't easy, as my French doesn't extend to words like plasticine. I was pretty clever though. They didn't have plasticine but did have Play Dough. That will do just as well I think. I will soften it up a bit so that you can get a good imprint."

"You got the right colour, I hope"

"I got red, that will be alright won't it?" She then realised I was making fun of her! For someone so intelligent she was so easy to catch out in this way.

"You Bastard."

We arrived for my lesson a good half hour early and parked next to the Ferrari. Colleen went into the office and started chatting to Bernadette, cleverly standing so that Bernadette had to turn, with her back to the car park.

I had a quick look round pretending to be interested in the lovely car. I casually knelt down by the front wheel on the driver's side of the Ferrari. The sort of thing anybody might do who was interested in sports cars.

Thank goodness the valve looked normal. Off with the dust cap and my stick fitted perfectly into the valve and down onto the pin. The whistle of escaping air from the tyre made me jump and I gritted my teeth and hoped it was not loud enough to attract attention, but as usual the place had its deserted look.

It only took a few seconds for the tyre to look really flat. I casually got up, then remembered the dust cap. Where the hell had I put the bloody thing. Thank God there it was, nearly under the deflated tyre which as it had flattened had partially covered the cap.

Now of course 'blondy' had to notice that she had a flat tyre as she walked out to get in.

I strolled back over to our van throwing my stick into the hedge as I got there. I put the small tin we had found for the Play Dough into my pocket, locked up the van and strolled on into the office, giving Colleen a wink as I walked in.

"Good afternoon, Bernadette, how are you today?" All said in my best French, this was about as good as it got.

Michel and 'blondy' soon came revving up outside in the Piper, now was the difficult bit of this little ploy.

A couple of minutes of friendly discussion between us all before 'blondy' left us and went out towards the car. We all watched her waggling bum walk away from us. Clothed today in emerald green. She really was quite a dish, but unbeknown to Michel we were watching for a very different reason than the thoughts that would be going through his

164

head; or not, in Colleen's case. I was able to think of two things at the same time!

She reached the car without appearing to notice the tyre, opened the door and got in. Hell, our little wicked scheme was not going to work.

The engine roared into life and we turned away. I thought that we must keep Michel here for as long as possible in the hope she would still come for assistance.

The Ferrari engine stopped, I turned to look back and could see that it had stopped after about ten yards. 'Blondy' had just got out and was looking at the tyre, she gave the tyre a kick, at the same time throwing her arms in the air in exasperation and we could see, but not hear, her swear roundly.

"Your girlfriend has a problem, Michel."

We all walked out towards the car.

"This is the last thing I needed, I have to be in Brest in half an hour and the breakdown people will take an age to get here." She raved.

This was of course all said in French and is my translation. Naturally, as I don't speak the language I couldn't understand any of it!

"Don't worry, I will soon change the tyre for you. You don't mind waiting a minute, do you Cris?"

"No of course not. Give me the keys and I will wander out to the plane and get settled in."

This was just perfect and all going as we had planned. So far so good.

"They are still in the ignition," Michel replied as he bent down over the car boot to get the spare tyre and tools out. Colleen grabbed the wheel brace and started to try and move the wheel nuts. I willed her not to help and speed up the wheel change. They were not in the pits of a car race for heaven's sake! I did not want to have to rush my job.

I strolled casually out to the plane, trying to give the impression that I was in no hurry at all; all rather an act as

165

I am sure nobody was taking any notice of me. I got in and settled in the seat, got the Play Dough tin out of my pocket and pushed each key carefully into the soft material so as to leave a clear impression. I gave the keys a good wipe on my handkerchief before putting them back in the ignition. Now what to do with the tin, it could very easily get damaged and the keys would then not fit the locks when we came to use them. Quickly thinking, I got out of the plane, being careful not to squeeze the tin lid too hard and squash the dough, and walked over to where Colleen was standing watching Michel from the office, having realised she could be of no help to him.

"Here, take this and keep it flat and out of the sun, in fact put it in the fridge in the van. I'm going to the loo."

I heard the snarl of the Ferrari engine again and the gravel of the car park being scattered as it accelerated away. Michel joined me in the loo to wash his hands.

"Another grateful pupil."

"I bet you wouldn't come and change my tyre. I am not nearly pretty enough!"

The lesson went off without anything remarkable happening. I rejoined Colleen who was sitting outside on the grass reading a book.

"Well that operation went off better than we could have hoped for. Tomorrow we had better get them over to our locksmith in Rennes."

Chapter 30

We left early the next morning for the long drive. Arriving mid morning we were able to park alongside the River Vilaine and walk on towards the magnificent cathedral to enquire the way to Rue St.Sauveur where the locksmith was located. This was part of the old town and a maze of narrow streets with houses with overhanging balconies, all most attractive. Monsieur Hubard, the locksmith, was tucked away at one end of the street.

"We rang two days ago about having keys cut from imprints, and you said bring the cast in to you."

Monsieur Hubard was a typical caricature of a Frenchman, starting with the beret on his head, cigarette stuck in one side of his mouth, (it could even have been a Gaulloise) set in a pale thin face. This was topped with straggling thinning hair peeping out from the beret, and wearing a rather grubby white bib apron.

He took the imprints, fumbled in his trouser pocket under the apron and pulled out a pair of pince nez spectacles. He then spent several minutes of close examination, during which puffs of smoke blew out of his nostrils, and he grunted quietly interspersed with deep sighs.

I could see Colleen trying to stop herself bursting into laughter, my hard nudge with my elbow did not seem to help matters. Personally I was too worried that after all this scrutiny he would say that it could not be done, that the imprint was not clear enough. If this was the case I couldn't think what we would do.

Colleen recovered her composure and quickly said "We are borrowing our friends' old car while we are over here for a few days, but they didn't want to lend us the keys as well as they will be coming over next week."

This was received as if he had not heard a word. It seemed a rather lame reason to me, but I certainly couldn't have thought up anything better on the spur of the moment, especially as car keys these days usually had a chip in them for the central locking. Eventually he gave a grunt followed by an even bigger puff of smoke.

He looked up over the top of the spectacles "Come back in two hours and they will be ready for you."

We spent that time most enjoyably wandering round the city and the superb cathedral with its colourful stained glass windows.

Sure enough Monsieur Hubard was as good as his word. The keys were ready, but I had a suspicion by the way he looked at us that he was not completely convinced by Colleen's explanation of this morning.

My sigh of relief was almost audible. This whole trip was playing hell with my nerves. Each stage was a new drama, but we had started out wanting excitement in our lives and were getting it by the bucketful.

We forked left for the road to Loudeac and Carhaix and decided to move campsite to Landivisiau, where we arrived quite late after a stop for supper.

Chapter 31

We woke fairly early. I got up and made us both a cup of tea and we just chatted light-heartedly for an hour lying in our bunks, as there was no hurry before what would be my last flying lesson this afternoon. Michel had told me he was happy for me to go solo next time and I felt that I had to move on now we had the keys. There was nothing to delay our departure. I was as confident as I was ever likely to be about the Channel flight.

This was a most attractive campsite right on the banks of the river Quillivarou on the eastern edge of the town. It was not too crowded with tents and mobile homes, but enough for ours not to stand out and be easily recalled in the event of any enquires. It looked as if it was going to be a lovely day. Earlier there had been a light mist hanging over the river, but this was now being sucked up as the heat of the sun, shining out of a clear blue sky, gradually increased. It was going to be another scorcher.

Today was the day. We needed a lot of things to go just right.

Colleen would not stay at the airfield while I had the lesson today. She would spend the time packing up our bags and cleaning the van as thoroughly as possible to leave no evidence of our identities, though we both realised that with modern forensics and DNA testing this was really an impossibility. It did cross my mind that my record might be on a database as a result of my military incarceration. It was too late to worry about that now. The other job which was of great importance was getting the cocaine out from all the various storage places and packing it into the boxes, which we had picked up from a hypermarket the day before. The police would soon connect the theft of the plane with our van and would realise that we were up to no good when they found the compartments I had constructed under the floor.

The idea was to pack 50 kilos in the boxes for the sale to Jo in Bristol and the other 50 kilos would be split between my backpack and grip holdall and Colleen's suitcase to go on to Stephen in London.

We wandered up into the town to the boulangerie to get croissants for breakfast. One of the best bits of France is the lovely fresh bread etc. that was so easy to get wherever you went. Across the road for paté and cheese for lunch, and we were set up for the day. No wine for either of us today. Hopefully it was going to be a long day and we could not afford to be drowsy.

A leisurely breakfast sitting outside in the sun. Oh, that life could be so uncomplicated. Good food, a pretty girl, hot sunshine, beautiful setting, what more could a bloke want? Perhaps when all this was over we could retire to a similar place with not a worry in the world. The present situation was of our choosing so who was I to complain?

We moved out, as holidaymakers might be expected to, a few kilometres down the road towards Landerneau and pulled into a side road which took us down to the river again. I took the opportunity to top up on my sleep bank for an hour, as it was going to be a long night.

Colleen dropped me off for the lesson in good time before driving off the way we had come.

Michel was still up with another pupil so I leant on the fence in front of the flying club busy with my own thoughts.

I felt a bit mean doing what I was doing to Michel. We had got on well together and he was a pleasant guy. I hoped his instructor's licence would not be at risk, though he could not really be blamed.

The Piper came in low over the boundary at the end of the strip and to my "professional" eye made a rather untidy heavy landing. I quite expected Michel to make his pupil go round again, as he had done with me a few days before, but instead they came bouncing across the grass towards me.

The same well-cut jeans encasing the same long legs and nicely rounded bum appeared, as the door was opened, followed by the rest, today in an expensive pale yellow shirt only buttoned down far enough to be just decent. It was a pity I was not to be around for a while to get to know her better. I did like the Ferrari, and it would have been fun to have had a ride. Perhaps she was on the same scam as us!

It was funny that we had never seen any other pupils when I had been for my lessons. It may have been that we were just at the beginning of the holiday season when the whole of France seems to come to a halt, or perhaps because we tended to come late in the day.

Michel gave me a slight wink from behind before saying in his broken English" I will be with you in a minute, as soon as I have booked Abigail in for her next lesson."

He joined me a moment later.

"I hope your wife doesn't know what you get up to with some of your pupils Michel!"

"Ah, you know what we French are like. L'amour and passion are like food for a hot blooded Frenchman, not like you cold and reserved English. Is the gorgeous Colleen not with you today"

"OK. Touché. No, she has gone back into town to do some shopping before picking me up again."

It was surprising how easy lying could become.

We strolled out to the Piper and I climbed up onto the

wing and inside. I don't think I will ever find getting in and out easy on these small planes.

Michel stood by the wing leaning inside the cabin.

"OK. Today's the day for going solo. Remember all that we have done in the lessons. Think twice before you commit to a manoeuvre, if you are not certain go round again to give yourself time. Keep a good look out for other aircraft. You are a good pilot Cris with a natural feel for the plane but don't be over confident. Good luck."

He slammed the door shut before I could say anything. Although I had done quite a lot of solo flying in the past I was really nervous about the events to come in the next few hours.

I was very relieved to see the fuel gauge showing just over half full. It was vital that we should be starting out tonight with the tank nearly half full, otherwise we might get our feet wet.

The flight went quickly, just practising a few turns and banks, restarting the engine after a cut out, flying by the instruments only, and general familiarisation with the aircraft. I don't think I will ever be a natural pilot, but at least I now felt I could cope with whatever occurred that night.

After twenty minutes I came back in to a very smooth touch down, which I was really proud of. I could show Abigail a thing or two!

Colleen was there waving as I came to a stop, playing the loving "wife" roll.

As I cut the engine she turned to Michel, "I do believe he is improving. That landing looked much better."

"Michel, I think I would like one more go solo, perhaps next week." I said, tongue in cheek knowing that all being well we would be miles away, and hopefully with a pocket full of money.

"Right, lets look at the diary. What about Tuesday, you

quite like the last lesson of the day, so what about 1600 like today."

"Fine by me, thanks and see you then."

"You've forgotten something, have you not?. Write up your log book and I will sign it." My heart missed a beat.

Colleen drove off slowly, while we both took one final look around to make sure we had imprinted in our minds the layout of the club, aircraft, and any other obstructions that could be a hazard tonight. It all looked too easy in daylight but would be quite different in the dark. The moon would, I think, still be very low when we planned to take off. Also there were some thundery-looking cumulus nimbus clouds coming up towards the south. It would be the last straw if today's heat turned to a thunder storm. No way would I fly in that sort of weather. Still we were not committed to going tonight, we had no fixed schedule to keep to. The question of the fuel was a slight worry. Assuming Michel was not flying again today which I thought very unlikely then I knew the plane had sufficient for our trip. If we had to postpone to another day we would not have any idea what was left in the tank until we broke in to go.

We returned to the campsite of last night, choosing a plot nearer to the entrance as we would be leaving again early.

"Let's walk up into the town shortly and try out that little restaurant we rather liked the look of the other day"

Colleen as usual was full of energy, or perhaps a bundle of nerves and unable to sit still for long.

"OK, but it must be a fairly alcohol-free evening for me, and I am not very happy about leaving the van out of our sight with all our goodies out of their hiding places and in the boxes, but I expect it will be alright."

The heat of the afternoon dissipated slightly as the sun began to sink. We strolled up to the town via the narrow little Rue St. Thivisiau with its attractively decorated fountain.

The restaurant/café was nearby, and was just open for business. I thought I could allow myself a Pernod, so we enjoyed these while Colleen chatted away to the patron in her excellent French only stumbling from time to time when the patron used local Brittany patois. It seemed to me that she had improved enormously since we had been there. For my part, I could only understand the odd word but was able to get the gist of what was being said. If pushed I could get along, but tended to let Colleen do the talking.

We decided to have the menu of the day with a bottle of Muscadet. An excellent meal, which we lingered over in true French fashion for awhile.

I took Colleen's arm as we wandered our way back to the campsite, she had drunk most of the wine and was definitely enjoying its effect. Talkative and totally relaxed. We sat in the fading light on the bank of the river before heading back to the van and turning in early.

I was just dozing off when Colleen crept into the bunk beside me. Her warm smooth naked body melding with mine as I turned over to face her. She snuggled her head into my shoulder, before raising herself to press her small firm breasts against my chest and with her hair falling down round my head finding my lips with hers for a long sweet kiss, our tongues deeply intertwined. Any ideas I might have had for a few hours sleep before we set off flew out of the window, my resistance was immediately nil as we explored each other's bodies, before she rolled on top of me and whispered "please now." I entered her slowly as heaven seemed to envelop me.

Chapter 32

After such passionate lovemaking there was little time left for sleep before we needed to set out.

"We must have more romantic dinners in future! That was a really good night luv."

"Don't get too carried away big boy, it was just the fact you made me finish up the wine" she said with a twinkle in her eye, but I could tell she had enjoyed it too. We left the campsite as planned at about eleven for the short drive into Landivisiau and on to the aerodrome. The centre of town was virtually deserted other than the odd young man making his way home. Landivisiau was not renowned for its vibrant nightlife. The road out of town was equally deserted and we arrived at the aerodrome entrance without meeting any traffic.

I stopped fifty yards down the road to clear my mind for the task ahead: "Let's just run through again what we have planned. "

"Oh, do we have to? Let's just get on with it. What if someone comes along and sees us?"

"It really would not matter two hoots. We will be connected with the missing plane as the van will be sitting right by the space the plane was in. If a car does come then it will be an excuse to have a cuddle. Come on one more go.

Run through the plan, I mean not the cuddle. Though God knows I could do with that just at the moment."

"All right. The door to the plane's cabin is on the starboard side. We drive up as near as possible so that the van can be left where we stop without being in the way of the tailplane as we move away. I have the keys to the cabin, get in and stow the boxes and our luggage inside the cabin as you pass them to me. Put them in behind the back seats and the holdall and your backpack on the back seat. This will spread the weight and balance the plane better."

"OK that's fine. While you're getting the door unlocked I start taking the boxes etc. from the van and, as soon as you're in, I pass them to you in double quick time. You will have put the keys in the ignition as you move across the cabin. You will then get out as quickly as possible to allow me into the cockpit."

"Right, it all sounds easy said like that. We've been over it so many times it must all work, but the best laid plans never go off as they should do."

"Don't be so pessimistic. It's not like you at all. It's going to go like clockwork."

I was trying to boost her confidence. Inside I was feeling just as nervous and at this moment would have been quite happy to call the whole thing off. The thought of the flying quite frankly scared the shit out of me.

"Let's go and put it into action."

We drove in through the entrance with the van lights off and as quietly as we could on round the little control tower to the line of parked aircraft. This was the real weak spot of this phase of the plan. We were certain the plane would be here, but would our keys fit the door, would there be sufficient fuel to complete the journey, would the engine starting and warming up waken someone who could stop us?

Would I, in my anxiety, get us off the ground!

Anyway, it was too late to worry now.

Past two Cessna 152's and a couple of others before three

Pipers with the flying club Piper Warrior nearly at the end of the row. It looked very small and fragile in the night glow, but with it we would complete the next stage.

I pulled up as planned. The adrenaline was really pumping now.

Colleen was out of the car like a greyhound, and crouching on the wing. She appeared to be having a moment's difficulty getting the key in the lock and turning it, as I could hear a muttered "Oh shit, come on you bloody thing." Probably it was just her nerves making her fumble. Then she had the door open and disappeared inside. I only had time to get one box out of the van and sitting on the wing before a muffled whisper of "Come on, get your finger out". I had not got out of the driving seat until I saw the door open, there seemed no point if the keys would not fit. What an impatient girl she was! No doubt like me she was a bundle of nerves. The sooner we were off the ground the happier we would both be.

The Piper was flown from the port seat so we had to do a quick swap round so that I could get in, no way was it possible to change over in the very small cabin. I suppose in an emergency when one was in the air it could be done, but under such circumstance one would try anything! Colleen had a quick check of the campervan while I scrambled up the plane's wing and over into my seat, pulling off the surgical gloves we had both been wearing since starting out from our final clean-up of the van.

I began on my pre-start checks with the aid of a small pocket torch. The ignition key turned quite easily. That was a relief. Lights flashed up on the dashboard. The magnetos appeared to be all right, the fuel tank was still just under half full, the lights on the radio came on (not that we would be using it unless there was an emergency like coming down in the sea.) and I slipped the headset over my head. The wheel and pedals felt OK and I could see the flaps moving up and down, I would just have to assume the rudder was moving.

177

The door clicked quietly shut and Colleen was strapping in beside me as I did likewise.

We looked at each other without saying a word. Colleen put her hand on my knee and gave it a squeeze and gave me a rather taut looking smile and mouthed what I took to be "let's get the hell out of here" but could have been anything. This was it.

I pressed the starter and the engine fired immediately, brakes off, a few revs on the engine to get us moving. We didn't budge an inch. Still more revs, nothing happening. The engine noise must be waking everybody for miles around. Another check of the brakes, they are definitely off.

Quick thinking as usual, Colleen said "I'll get out and see if there is anything tying us down" She had the door open in a flash and was scrambling out onto the wing again when, thank goodness, I realised that in her rush and anxiety to get us going she might easily have forgotten about the propeller revolving at high speed as just a blur in front of us.

"Mind the propeller" I shouted as loud as I could over the noise of the engine and at the same time reached forward to push the throttle lever hard shut and the engine subsided to tick over. She turned towards me and gave me a startled look, which told me she hadn't thought of it, followed by a thumbs up, before disappearing from my sight under the wing. What a dreadful tragedy it would have been if she hadn't heard me. Everything had gone so well up to this point and that sort of thing had never crossed our minds.

Ten seconds later she was scrambling up the wing again into her seat.

"Try it now, there were chocks under the wheels stopping us rolling forward." She said rather breathlessly as she refastened her seat belt.

Throttle slightly open again and we started to roll forward. It's amazing how a little thing like two pieces of wood could have scuppered the whole operation, not to mention killing Colleen instantly if she had run forward.

No time for a warm-up of the engine now, it was get up and go time as quickly as possible. There was no wind to speak of so I wasn't going to worry about taxiing to get downwind. As soon as we were onto the grass strip and lined up, it was full throttle and we quickly picked up speed bouncing over the slightly uneven surface before making one last hop, and we were airborne.

There had been no interference and no sign of life as we left, but the engine noise must have alerted someone and the plane's disappearance would be reported very shortly.

I turned rather tentatively onto our course of 28 degrees East, straining my eyes all the time to keep a view of the ground which flashed by beneath us. I hoped that I wasn't flying high enough to be picked up on radar, not that I had the faintest idea what height that might be. Equally we didn't want to scrape the top of a tree. Our recce had discovered that there was no noticably high ground or electricity cables between the air strip and the coast, so that was one less worry.

"Keep your eyes on the ground ahead and shout if you see anything." I said rather unnecessarily as she was hunched forward in her seat as far as the restraint of the seat belt would allow, just as I was.

Moonlight was just beginning to show through a large bank of cloud to starboard, but it was quite difficult to keep the horizon in view. Was it going to be any easier once we got over the sea? I really should be flying on the instruments rather than by the seat of my pants.

"No, keep a good look out on your side rather than to the front, this is much more difficult than flying in daylight. It's impossible to tell how high we are."

"You were quite confident about it yesterday. Up, up, we seemed terribly close to those trees."

I dragged back on the wheel and we rose quickly before I levelled off again. I was not enjoying this one little bit. I had felt quite confident flying with Michel in daylight, but now had lost confidence in myself. This was a different kettle of fish. I cheered myself up with the thought that it must be easier over the sea. Thank goodness for the bit of moonlight. All these flashes rushed through my head one after the other. I suppose it was all part of my intense concentration.

About ten minutes after take off we got our first glimpse of the sea to port, and shortly after the lights of Roscoff to starboard, and then the sea was below us.

I dropped down lower to what I hoped was about 100 feet, or so the altimeter told me. We now had about an hour and a half before reaching the coast of Devon.

I could relax a little more at this stage. The moon came fully out, nearly behind us, and picked out a silvery path on the water that seemed to say "just follow me to your landfall". It was certainly easier now there was more light and I knew there were no obstacles in the way, provided there were no big ships with high masts, but we should have time to see them in this light.

"Well, you didn't do badly back there," Colleen said. "I feel happier being over the sea with some light, I must say. It was rather hairy flying over the land. We were jolly close to those trees. I would not be surprised to find we have a load of leaves stuck to the wheels. I nearly wet myself."

"You're not the only one. I nearly had a heart attack when we wouldn't move and I really thought you were going to run into the propeller. Apart from the mess it would have made, I would have been more than sorry to have lost you after all we have been through." A quick glance to my right and I could see she had understood the meaning behind my words.

"On the other hand, I wouldn't have had to share the cash with you!" I said trying to relax us both.

"Trust you to joke about it and spoil what you said before."

At this stage of the operation it was no time to be getting

extra feelings for each other. After all we were just business partners, and perhaps a bit more.

"Would you like a cup of coffee? I've got a flask in the back."

"That sounds a really good idea, I don't suppose you have a nice home-made cake as well?" I got the sort of reaction that I had been expecting. Her tongue stuck out at me as she turned and reached into the back. Colleen was not the most talented of girls in the haute cuisine department.. I had had experience of this over the course of the last few months.

The time seemed to fly by with very little to see except the lights of a few ships making their way along the Channel. We were flying without lights so probably they had no idea we were there. They would be unlikely to hear us from their enclosed bridges.

We kept off the subject of the operation and, other than the odd comment about the sky and stars, just sat back and enjoyed the trip. It would very soon need all our attention again.

Chapter 33

———

"That's it. Those must be the lights of Exmouth straight ahead of us, and that's Torbay just showing through the mist. We've made quite a good landfall. In fact we are spot on. More luck than skill and we have been lucky there is no wind to speak of to have blown us off course too far."

Sure enough the River Exe estuary came into sight on our left-hand side. We were a little further east than I had hoped for, but the light breeze at take off had been from the south west so we had probably been pushed up Channel slightly during the crossing. Navigation was certainly not one of my strong points. I had set the compass at our course of 28 degrees East when we were airborne and we had used our own hand-held GPS to check our position from time to time as we had made the crossing. GPS was illegal if used in an aircraft, but we were far more illegal in other respects, so this was a very minor detail! Come to that, I was not qualified for night flying either. In for a penny in for a pound!

I could feel Colleen, sitting next to me, shivering with excitement or more probably nervousness, it certainly was not with cold as it was pretty warm and stuffy in the little cabin and the outside temperature would not be too low on a fine summer's night. I certainly felt very tensed up again, but the concentration of flying and wondering whether the next stage of the plan would go off all right gave me little time to dwell on the risks we were taking, flying at 100 feet over the sea. In the middle of the night, in a relatively unfamiliar plane. This was quite enough to get the adrenaline flowing.

I turned slowly to port to try and keep to the centre of the estuary and gain a little height. The last thing we needed was to get mixed up in a flock of geese or other birds, but low enough not to get snarled up with air traffic in or out of Exeter airport a few miles to our right. I didn't expect any at this time of night. Very quickly the estuary gave way to the river and the lights of Exeter.

"There's the motorway straight ahead. Not a lot of traffic but plenty to give us leading lights."

The M5 crosses the river and canal on a very obvious bridge and was a very good checkpoint to establish our exact position. It was our next lead to take us into the heart of Devon. The traffic on the motorway never stops and the succession of lights was like a well-lit runway. A quick look at the fuel gauge showed that we should have plenty of juice provided we could land straight in and didn't have to spend time searching for the gliding field, which would of course be unlit. If there was not enough then there was going to be a big bump! The field could look rather like any other field from above. Colleen had not made particular note of features during her brief flight in the glider; she had been too excited.

I was now on fairly familiar territory, but it all looked very different by night. Why on earth did I ever start in on this thing I said to myself for the hundredth time. If we missed this turning point we would end up at Bristol unless the fuel ran out first.

"Those must be the lights of Broadclyst and the ones to the left of the motorway, Bradninch. Now we turn north east before we get to Cullompton onto a fixed bearing of, what was it?"

"Cris for God's sake, it's 40 degrees. Can't you remember anything?"

Thank goodness Colleen still had her wits about her; my mind had gone a complete blank.

We no longer had any definite points of reference to follow, other than the compass course. We had planned this bit of the operation as best we could on the ground and had chosen the timing to coincide with the full moon, so had done all that was possible pre flight. But we still had to pick up the steeply rising escarpment of the Blackdowns, where we had admired the view so much when we were checking out the gliding field. At that time we had had no idea what plane we would be flying and so had not been able to calculate the flight time from the motorway, but it was going to be only a very few minutes. We had been gaining height all the way up the motorway, but the final approach was over a sudden rise of at least 100 meters in the space of half a mile, if I got it wrong there would be a nasty splat. Our height now should be sufficient to give us a couple of hundred feet over the hills. That was assuming the contour lines on the map had been accurate and that I had read them correctly.

"There, there's the gap between the trees on the end of the hill." And a moment later: "Those are the three big beech trees to the right of the landing strip."

Thank goodness for Colleen's sharp young eyesight. I had been concentrating much more on what was immediately in front of us and trying to keep to our bearing. The plane, or I, seemed to have a tendency to drift to port and gain height as I worried about the hills.

This was great, to have picked out the gliding field on our approach with no need even to do a circuit, let alone having to search for it. Fuel would be OK and we would even have enough to make several attempts at landing if I kept getting it wrong.

At this moment I felt the gods were with us as the moon came completely out from behind a small cloud and we had full clear moonlight. I just hoped that they would continue to smile on us for the next few minutes while we landed. Now I could focus on the edge of the field so as to touch down and stop as quickly as possible.

Where was the tractor winch used by the gliding club? That must be it. The dark lump over to the left. OK, we have a clear run in. We were both silent, gripping our seats tightly.

Right there is the top of the slope and I could now glimpse the edge of the grass running away in front for as far as I could see in the gloaming. What the hell is that white patch just off to the left. Oh shit, it is a flock of sheep. I had not expected anything like that. OK, they are running the right way and are not a problem…

I made one of my better touchdowns with only a couple of hops before gravity took over and we stuck to the ground. I gunned the engine lightly and we rolled on, to stop as close up to the trees on the west side as possible. We had decided that this was the best place to park up, well away from the clubhouse. Hopefully the plane might not be noticed for a few hours, or even days, parked right out away from the centre of activity. I had considered setting fire to it so as to try and hide its identity. However this would have been like lighting a beacon which someone would be bound to report with the inevitable investigation and enquiry. This way at the worst we should get a few hours of get-away time. I also felt sorry for Michel who had been very pleasant to us, if we just left it he would at least get it back some time.

"Well done. I am glad that is over. It was a very neat landing. Michel would be proud of you!"

No time now to hang around other than a quick stretch and a sigh of relief.

"Right, let's get the show on the road. You remember where we parked the car and you've got the ignition key?"

"Of course I bloody well have, I've been checking every few minutes since we left France"

185

"You have about half a mile to the car and for heavens sake keep it quiet. There are bound to be a few people in caravans who may have heard us come in. The last thing we need is some nosy parker do-gooder coming over to see what we are doing. I'll start getting the "cargo" unloaded."

I could still easily see Colleen in the moonlight at 100 meters so I just hoped there were no insomniacs walking their dogs at this time of night. It was quite a relief to get out of the plane so I had a quick walk round to check the lie of the land and loosen up before getting the boxes and bags out from the rear seats and baggage space.

In what seemed a very short time Colleen was back with the car. "You must have run. I hope nobody saw you cavorting across the grass"

"Oh yes, of course I had plenty of time for a quick shag with a couple of handsome young men on the way. Anyway the car started first go. I was afraid I might sit there winding the starter over for ages or the battery be flat."

We were both, I think, feeling rather light-headed at having survived what was another of the more dangerous few hours of the operation. The unpredictable bits were now all over; the rest was all planned with our buyers in place.

The boxes of cocaine went in the car boot. They certainly squashed the springs down more than I had expected. The suitcase and backpack, along with our coats, we chucked casually on the back seat; the idea being that should we be stopped or have to talk to someone as we left the field, it would just look as if we were going home after a few days" gliding, even if it was the early morning. After all, the car had been parked here for several days and might be familiar.

"Will you drive for a bit, luv. Now we are on terra firma again, I could do with a spell away from having to concentrate."

"OK, but just stay awake long enough to get us out of this maze of lanes. I'll probably remember the way, but I should hate to get stuck down some farmer's muddy track with this lot on board."

It seemed a pity to be just abandoning the plane, which had served its part so well.

We took it pretty steady over the grass, without any lights on, until we got to the tarmac by the clubhouse. No sign of lights anywhere, and we were able to speed up down the driveway between the ancient wind-blown beech trees, before we turned onto the road which would take us through to Taunton and then up the motorway to Bristol and home. We planned to have a couple of days' relaxation before we contacted our buyers, although I would feel a lot happier once we were rid of the cocaine.

"You turn right at the end and then left. I think you will remember it as we go along, though one cannot see familiar landmarks in the dark. Anyway it will start to get light before too long."

I slouched down in the passenger seat confident that Colleen would take over now.

Chapter 34

I quickly dropped off to sleep but it seemed immediately that Colleen gave me a nudge. I looked up and realised that we had only gone two or three miles.

"Blimey, give me a break. I had only just dropped off and was just into a nice dream……"

"Do shut up a minute. There's a car coming up fast behind us. What do I do, slow down and let him past?"

"Yes, I should. It may be someone late for an early shift or even rushing the wife to hospital. Certainly not worth waking me up for."

A moment later the following car's lights swept across us as it came close up behind as we rounded a corner. It made no attempt to overtake in spite of Colleen pulling over to the near side as far as possible and the road looked clear ahead.

"They're not coming by, it's just sitting right up close on our bumper. Come on past you bastards. What the hell are you playing at? Oh God, that's a police car pulled across the road, and the car behind has put on its flashing blue light."

"As if I hadn't noticed. OK, keep calm let's see if we can bluff this one out. How could they possibly know why we are here. They are probably doing a routine check of all traffic at this early time of the morning. Your sweetest smile, and for once don't slag them off."

"Oh yes. Pretty funny that they have two cars in just the right place on this minor road."

Colleen pulled carefully into the verge behind the car in front while the other police car pulled in close behind. Two figures in yellow reflective jackets walked round, from the car in front, one to each side as Colleen lowered her window.

"Good morning officer, how can we help?"

This was certainly a Colleen I had not seen for quite a long time, in fact since we crossed the Portuguese/ Spanish border, as if she was greeting one of her customers for the first time. All charm and sweetness.

"Good morning, madam. Have you just come from the gliding field?"

"Yes, we have been having a few days gliding but have to be back in London early for work."

"Do you both mind stepping out of the car please, and opening the boot."

My heart sank into my boots as I walked round to do as asked. We had been rumbled for sure, unless it was chance they were looking for something else, but as Colleen had said that was pretty unlikely. This was the end of the line after all our effort. They knew we were coming. Who the hell grassed on us? Anyway, there would be plenty of time for reflection over the next few years. I was feeling utter dejection. It had all gone so well up to now.

As I rounded the back of the car I couldn't help feeling that this didn't seem quite like the way the police should have been behaving if this was a real bust, or as shown on a TV drama.

Sure enough, as I got to the back I could see by the lights of the car behind what looked remarkably like a hand gun pointed at my stomach by one of the two men who had got out of the car behind. The car was white, but with no insignia or marking of any kind on it. Its blue light had now disappeared and these two guys were wearing what looked like bomber jackets and balaclavas. In no way were these police. Who the hell were they, though?

Colleen appeared from the driver's side escorted by the two in their reflective jackets, each firmly holding her by the elbow. As the situation sank in she let fly with a remarkable mixture of gutter Irish interspersed with what sounded like gutter Colombian. The like of which I had never heard even in the Army. She certainly had spirit, and if the situation hadn't been so serious it would have been laughable.

"Shut it girl, or you will get a mouth full of this" as he waved a gun under her nose. "Nobody's going to hear you out here, but I don't like being slagged off by a tart like you."

I am not very good on regional accents, but this voice sounded very Brummy, which helped us not one iota.

"Colleen, don't do anything violent, it's not worth it. We've been set up." I said in as cool a voice as possible, but absolutely seething inside.

"That is certainly true. I should hate to spoil that pretty face."

One of the men cut the string on one of the boxes and peered in using a pencil torch.

"Looks OK , as far as I can tell without slitting a bag. There's six bags in each box and four boxes, no wait a minute, this one has seven, so that's the lot. Do you want me to slit a bag and try it?"

This voice could have been East London.

"No don't bother. If it's not the stuff we know where to find them."

I wondered briefly what they would do with us now, assuming they would grab the cocaine. I wasn't too hopeful that it wouldn't be rather messy. Drug dealers were not renowned for their gentle habits. They more often shot first before discovering who they had killed. There was too much money involved and in this case they had got a couple of suckers who had done all the work and put the money up front. It was money for old rope for them.

We were just a couple of amateurs up against professionals.

I had had these fears when we were making our sale to Stephen in London. Were these a "Yardie" gang? But they were usually Jamaicans. It did not really matter to us now.

I did not have to wait long to find out.

We were blindfolded and my hands tied behind my back, before I was bundled into one of the "police" cars, still with a gun stuck in my ribs, by the man who seemed to be the leader. I could hear and feel what I assumed was the transferring of the boxes from our car to theirs, then one of them got in the driver's seat and we moved off. I just hoped that Colleen had been treated alright. She had quietened down somewhat and was perhaps in the other car. She didn't deserve being abused or beaten up in any way. The men seemed to have known our exact movements, so I assumed they must know our backgrounds as well and would be aware that Colleen had worked in the oldest profession and might take advantage of this to rape her before disposing of her body. So I just hoped she would realise the seriousness of our situation.

I had not caught sight of any of their faces so we might be lucky, but the drug fraternity were not renowned for their leniency. Who could possibly have set us up? One of the Gonzales? Captain Zacapa? Jo or Stephen? But none of them knew what our plans were, in fact we had not known what our plans were ourselves, so how could it possibly be any of them. All these thoughts rushed through my head. Could it possibly be Colleen? The idea struck home like a hammer blow.

But she had not had any opportunity to contact anybody since arriving at Oporto, we had always been together.

I suppose she could have had some sort of direction finder beacon that could be followed.

No, I trusted her, she would never do that to me.

Anyway, I had no intention of asking her as it would

completely ruin any close relationship we might have built up. If I survived the next few hours then all I would have lost would be quite a lot of money, but still have her.

Would I actually want to be together with her if I had this suspicion? Probably not.

If it was not her, then she would probably be having just the same suspicions about me as I was having about her. It really didn't matter at the moment. Quite likely nothing would matter soon.

Ten minutes later the car stopped, the door opened and I was pushed out into the road, landing awkwardly on my right shoulder and giving my forehead a crack on the ground. I struggled to rub off the blindfold on the ground and watched as two sets of rear lights disappeared up the road.

At the same moment I heard with great relief Colleen start up again very tearfully, "the bloody rotten buggers, how could they do this after all we've been through and the money and effort we have put into it"

"Are you alright? Can you come and undo my hands" I asked tentatively.

"No, I'm feeling just bloody wonderful having lost a potential 200k's worth of money. What about you?" said with all the invective and anger possible. Personally at the moment I just felt relief that I was alive, in spite of what felt like blood running down into my right eye.

"Calm down and come here and let's try and decide what to do now. Let's get these ropes off our wrists."

We stood back to back and were able each to undo the other's bindings.

Colleen's mood changed in an instant and as I turned she came into my arms and started to cry floods of tears.

"I was so afraid on my own and thought they were going to shoot us. Oh, look at your head, it's pouring blood. What did they do to you, Cris? Have you got a hanky, let me mop you up."

This was the Colleen, I realised I had become really very

fond of as a person, rather than as a colleague, or as one of her lovers when I had met her first which seemed an age ago.

"They did nothing to me except tie me up and push me out of the car just now. I suppose I cut my head when I cracked it on the ground. So what now? Find a phone and report our loss to the police!"

"Don't be so bloody stupid." The change of mood again until she realised I was trying to cheer her up. Whereupon I received a punch in the ribs, for my effort, as she pulled away.

"Right, we were only in the car for about ten minutes and we came from that direction, so let's start walking and see if we can find our car, as we know roughly where we were when we were mugged."

I didn't recall any sharp turns at junctions and felt once I could get my whereabouts we had a good chance of getting back to the car.

An hour later we did just that. It was still pulled into the side of the road as we had left it with the keys still in the ignition. What's more, on the back seat under our coats was the suitcase, my backpack, and the holdall.

We hadn't lost everything. The wisdom of splitting the cocaine into two lots for sale had proved well worth doing. Whoever had robbed us was only expecting 50 kilos and had not bothered to look any further. This anyway proved that my uncharitable thoughts about Colleen being involved were completely unfounded, and almost certainly the Gonzales family. Fredericko knew how much we had, but the boys could still be in the frame.

The value of what we had left would be plenty to grease a few palms to discover who had robbed us.

But that could wait for another day.

David Barrow was born in Surrey in 1935. During the war years the family evacuated to Scotland and back to Sussex. School at Rannoch in Scotland / Broadstairs in Kent. His education was completed at Charterhouse in Surrey. Two years National Service was done in the Royal Navy, getting a commission as a Midshipman serving mostly in minesweepers. During this time he was selected to represent the navy at swimming. Agriculture was always his ambition and on being "demobed" he completed a two-year course in agriculture at Cirencester, Glos. After 9 years of farm management he and his wife acquired a farm in Dorset. Thirty years on, the farm was sold and they moved to East Devon into "semi-retirement" running a successful tree nursery business. A succession of hip replacements forced a second retirement and the writing of this first novel. They have been married for 48 years, have 3 children and 6 grandchildren.

ISBN 141209063-6